Daniel Wise

The Young Man's Counsellor

Or, sketches and illustrations of the duties and dangers of young men: designed to

be a guide to success in this life, and to happiness in the life which is to come

Daniel Wise

The Young Man's Counsellor
Or, sketches and illustrations of the duties and dangers of young men: designed to be a guide to success in this life, and to happiness in the life which is to come

ISBN/EAN: 9783337097042

Printed in Europe, USA, Canada, Australia, Japan

Cover: Foto ©Andreas Hilbeck / pixelio.de

More available books at **www.hansebooks.com**

THE

YOUNG MAN'S COUNSELOR;

OR,

Sketches and Illustrations

OF

THE DUTIES AND DANGERS

OF

YOUNG MEN.

DESIGNED TO BE A GUIDE TO SUCCESS IN THIS LIFE, AND TO
HAPPINESS IN THE LIFE WHICH IS TO COME.

BY REV. DANIEL WISE, A. M.,

AUTHOR OF "THE PATH OF LIFE," "BRIDAL GREETINGS," "LIFE OF
ZWINGLE," ETC.

Cincinnati:

PUBLISHED BY POE & HITCHCOCK,

FOR THE METHODIST EPISCOPAL CHURCH, AT THE WESTERN BOOK
CONCERN, CORNER OF MAIN AND EIGHTH STREETS.

R. P. THOMPSON, PRINTER.

1862.

TO

THE YOUNG MEN OF AMERICA

𝕿𝖍𝖎𝖘 𝕭𝖔𝖔𝖐

IS AFFECTIONATELY INSCRIBED,

BY

THEIR SINCERE FRIEND AND WELL-WISHER

DANIEL WISE.

Preface.

I LOVE to look upon a young man. There is a hidden potency concealed within his breast which charms and pains me. I silently ask, What will that youth accomplish in the aftertime of his life? Will he take rank with the benefactors or with the scourges of his race? Will he, erewhile, exhibit the patriotic virtue of Hampden and Washington, or the selfish craftiness of Benedict Arnold? If he have genius, will he consecrate it, like Milton and Montgomery, to humanity and religion; or, like Moore and Byron, to the polluted altars of passion? If he have mercantile skill, will he employ it, like Astor or Girard, to gratify his lust of wealth; or to elevate and bless humanity, like some of our living merchant princes? If the gift of eloquence be hidden in his undeveloped soul, will he use it, like Summerfield, in favor of religion, or, like Patrick Henry and Adams, in battling for human rights; or will he, for mammon's sake, prostitute that gift to the uses of tyranny and infidelity? Will that immortal soul, which beams with intelligence and power in his countenance, ally itself with its Creator, and thus rise to the sublime hight of its destiny; or will it wage war with truth and duty, and thus sink to degradation and to death? As I raise these great queries I at once do reverence to the high potentiality of his nature, and tremble for his fate. I feel a desire arising within me to bear a.part in guiding him into the way of right, duty, and happiness. As a fruit of that 'often-felt desire, I have written this book. May its success equal the ardor and sincerity of my wishes for the best good of young men!

DANIEL WISE.

Fall River, November, 1850.

Contents.

CHAPTER I.
YOUTHFUL DAY-DREAMS DISSOLVED.

The young man invited to view the future—A joyous thought—
A young man's dream of life—Disenchantment—The sower and
the harvest—The young man a sower in the field of life—The two
harvests—To be a young man a very serious fact—Sailing on a
quiet river and steering through dangerous straits—The enchanted
hill—Life an enchanted hill, with many victims—Every young
man who falls is his own destroyer—The Alpine muleteer and the
meditative man—An enemy at home—The asp—The young man's
complaint anticipated—Caution the parent of success—Napoleon's
forecast—Dupont's incaution—The defeat at Baylen—Every young
man may conquer the obstacles of life—The young man should
cheerfully contend for success—Alcinou's Garden.

CHAPTER II.
THE CORNER-STONE OF A SUCCESSFUL LIFE.

The stately mansion—Its ruin—The owner's folly—Every young
man is constructing a character—Its materials—Importance of a
right foundation—Building on the sand—Ruin—The true foundation of right character—The temporal advantages of a religious
life—Prosperity not the exclusive heritage of worldlings—Benefits
of religion—The lovely charmer and her promises—Religion not
the only path to temporal good—Worldlings prosper without it—
No tranquillity to mere worldlings—Confessions of Voltaire—Chesterfield—Lord Byron—Nelson—Talleyrand—Randolph—An affecting contrast—Religious life preferable to one of profitable sin—
Extract—An illustration—The poisoned water—Specifics—The
poisoned heart—The genius of the world and religion—The choice

CHAPTER III.

INTEGRITY NECESSARY TO SUCCESS IN LIFE.

CHAPTER IV.

INTELLIGENCE AN ELEMENT OF A SUCCESSFUL LIFE.

CHAPTER V.

ENERGY AN ELEMENT OF DISTINCTION.

CHAPTER VI.

INDUSTRY THE HIGHWAY TO SUCCESS.

CHAPTER VII.

ECONOMY AND TACT.

CHAPTER VIII.

HARMONY OF CHARACTER.

CHAPTER IX.

VICE AND ITS ALLUREMENTS.

CHAPTER X.

VICE AND ITS CONSEQUENCES.

CHAPTER XI.

VICE AND ITS SEDUCERS.

CHAPTER XII.

COURTSHIP AND MARRIAGE.

THE

𝔜𝔬𝔲𝔫𝔤 𝔐𝔞𝔫'𝔰 ℭ𝔬𝔲𝔫𝔰𝔢𝔩𝔬𝔯.

CHAPTER I.

YOUTHFUL DAY-DREAMS DISSOLVED.

GIVE me your hand, my dear young friend, and I will lead you to the dark passages and the rugged steeps, whose forbidding shadows fall gloomily on the highway of life. I will also conduct you to the green and sunny spots whereon you may indulge in innocent delights. Open your heart to my counsels. I will teach you how to escape the teeming dangers which, like troops of ill-omened phantoms, wait in the "slippery places" of youth, seeking his destruction. I will unfold to you the secrets of success and of eminence in this life, and the sure means of winning a crown of glory in the next.

It is, without doubt, a very joyous thought to

13

you that you have become a young man. Manhood has long been the fairy-land of your boyhood's reveries. Your full heart swells, as you exclaim:

> "Time on my brow hath set his seal;
> I start to find myself a man."

Your spirits flow in rich currents of feeling, and your lively imagination paints the most inviting pictures of the future. To you, life is as the lovely vale of Arno, with its enchanting scenery of groves and gardens, grottoes, palaces, and towers; its transparent lakes, delicious air, and sunny skies. You can comprehend the poet, who says:

> "To sanguine youth's enraptured eye,
>   Heaven has its reflex in the sky,
>   The winds themselves have melody,
>   Like harp some seraph sweepeth;
>   A silver decks the hawthorn bloom,
>   A legend shrines the mossy tomb,
>   And spirits throng the starry gloom,
>   Her reign when midnight keepeth."

It seems a pity to dim so fair a vision. I feel sad, as I proceed to break the sweet enchantment, and by touching it with the wand of truth, to overcast it with clouds and storms. But I should not be a faithful friend if I did not assure you that these rosy anticipations are destined to be followed by disappointment. You must and will learn the truthfulness of the following sweetly-solemn strain:

> "Little we dream, when life is new,
>   And nature fresh and fair to view,
>   When throbs the heart to pleasure true,
>   As if for naught it wanted—
>   That year by year, and ray by ray,
>   Romance's sunlight dies away,
>   And long before the hair is gray
>   The heart is disenchanted."

Let us walk forth into the fields, and learn a lesson from yonder husbandman. He is casting handfuls of seed broadcast upon the upturned soil. A moment's reflection teaches you that very much of the forthcoming harvest depends upon that sower and his seed. If he has properly chosen and prepared the soil; if the seed be of high quality; if it be sown in proper quantity, and harrowed with all due skill, the conditions of a good and abundant harvest are fulfilled, and may be reasonably expected. But if he has scantily sown poor seed in an ungenial and neglected soil, a good harvest is out of the question. The application of this figure to yourself is easy. You are now a sower of seed on the field of life. These bright days of youth are the seed-time. Every thought of your intellect, every emotion of your heart, every word of your tongue, every principle you adopt, every act you perform, is a seed, whose good or evil fruit will be the bliss or bane of your aftertime. As is the seed, so will be the crop. Indulge your appetites, gratify your passions, neglect your intellect, foster wrong principles, cherish habits of idleness, vulgarity, dissipation, and in the after years of manhood you will reap a plentiful crop of corruption, shame, degradation, and remorse; and, it may be,

> " Year by year, alone
> Sit brooding in the ruins of a life,
> Nightmare of youth, the specter of *yourself.*"

But if you control your appetite, subdue your

passions, firmly adopt and rigidly practice right principles, form habits of purity, propriety, sobriety, and diligence, your harvest will be one of honor, health, happiness; and

> " Aftertime,
> And that full voice which circles round the grave,
> Will rank you nobly."

That you have reached the period of youth, is, therefore, for you, a very *serious* fact. " Great destinies lie shrouded" in your swiftly-passing hours. Great responsibilities stand in the passages of every-day life. Great dangers lie hidden in the by-paths of life's great highway; and sirens, whose song is as charming as the voice of Calypso, are there to allure you to destruction. Great uncertainty hangs over your future history. God has given you existence, with full power and opportunity to improve it, and be happy. He has given you equal power to despise the gift, and be wretched. Which you will do, is the grand problem to be solved by your choice and conduct. To you, so young, so inexperienced, sc susceptible of evil, so capable of good, so full of

2

stormy feelings, so unsettled in opinion, is committed the awful trust of your future happiness.
Your bliss or misery, in two worlds, hangs poised
in the balance. The manner in which you spend
your youth will turn the scale for weal or for woe.
Verily it has been well said, that the season of
youth is a *critical* period. Critical, indeed! And
I would, if possible, engrave the thought, in inef-
faceable letters, on your susceptible heart, and
make you feel how much the fashioning of your
destiny, which hitherto has been more in the
hands of others than in your own, is now confided
to your discretion. —

As a boy, at home, you have sailed upon the
calm waters of a quiet river, in a bark carefully
furnished by a mother's love, and safely guided by
a father's skill. Now you are sailing through the
winding channels, the rocky straits, the rapid,
rushing currents, at the river's mouth, into tho
great sea of active life. And here, for the first
time, you are in *command* of the vessel. On *your*
skill and caution depends the safety of the passage. Neglect the rules laid down on the chart

of experience by previous navigators, take passion for a pilot, place folly at the helm, and your bark wil. shortly lie a pitiful wreck on the rocks, or be so damaged as to peril your safety on the coming voyage.   But study well the intricacies and dangers of your course, take counsel of experience, let caution be your pilot, and, without doubt, you will escape rock, current, eddy, and whirlpool, and, with streamered masts and big white sail, float gayly forth to dare and conquer the perils of the sea beyond.

Among the fascinating stories of the Orientals is one which describes an enchanted hill, whose summit concealed an object of incomparable worth.   It was offered as a prize to him who should ascend the hill without looking behind him.   But whoever ventured to secure this treasure was told that, if he did look backward, he should be instantly changed into a stone.   Many a princely youth, allured by the tempting prize, had ventured up that fatal hill; and as many had been changed to stones.   For the adjacent groves were filled with most melodious voices, and with birds

of sweetest song, whose bewitching strains and
enticements followed each youth as he ascended,
till he suffered his innate curiosity to control his
hopes and fears — turned his head, and instantly
became a stone. Hence, said the story, the hill-
side was covered with stones.

To every young man, life is such an enchanted
hill, with its thousands of alluring voices and its
unnumbered victims, who, prompted from within
themselves, have listened to some fatal charmer
of the senses, and have perished. Yet no one
of them ever fell of necessity. Had they re-
pressed the inward desire of evil, by directing
the energy of their souls after the great prizes
of religion and virtue, they would have become
conquerors; for *outward* things have power only
in proportion to the disposition of the mind to
be affected by them. Why, for example, does
the sublime and beautiful scenery of the Alps
awaken no emotions of beauty or sublimity in the
breast of the muleteer, whose life is spent in traversing their passages? And why does that same
scenery hold the reflective and religious mind in

rapt admiration? The answer is simple, but significant. Between nature and the muleteer there
exists no sympathy. He is hardened against her.
But the soul of the meditative and cultivated man
is in harmony with her charms. Hence, over the
former she has no power while she inspires the
latter with rapture. So with the charms of vice;
they fall powerless upon minds which, cased in
the mail of virtue, are proof against them; but
they are omnipotent to those whose undisciplined
passions are looking out upon life with prurient
curiosity. Such young men are doomed to illustrate the fable of the orient, and to lie along the
highways of life, hardened, undone, and lost.

The young man can not, therefore, fail to see
that he carries the most potent of all sources of
danger in his own breast. Within himself, as the
malignant asp lay concealed in the basket of
flowers brought to Cleopatra, lies his destroyer.
Unless you suffer your own passions to exercise
lordship over your reason and conscience, you can
not be greatly harmed. But herein lies your peril,
at the present epoch of your life. Passion is

strong, because reason is weak; desire eager, because it must not be gratified. Your heart is a
volcano of feeling, ever heaving, and seeking,
especially when in presence of the outward
tempter, to overflow your life with vice and abomination. There is a disposition in your soul to
respond to the fatal voices which solicit your
senses to trespass upon forbidden grounds. And
herein — I solemnly repeat it — lies your most
imminent danger.

These views are certainly sufficient to dim the
luster of those day-dreams of life, so natural and
so universal in young men. · Perhaps you consider
them too somber and gloomy in their aspects.
You complain that I have dipped my pen in the
too sober hues of autumn, when I ought to have
written with the bright drops which sparkle like
jewels on the gay blossoms and painted flowers
of spring; that I have caused you to despond,
when I should have stimulated your hopes and
excited your courage. But such is not my inten-
tion, nor should aught I have said occasion the
least despondency; it should only awaken caution;

caution, the parent of safety, the companion of success. Know you not that dangers are not to be overcome by blindly rushing among them? The wisest and best men are they who, like the greatest generals, take distinct cognizance of their dangers, and prepare with proper forecast to overcome them. Napoleon, that great master of war, never failed to calculate upon, and to provide beforehand for every imaginable difficulty. Had his lieutenant, the unfortunate General Dupont, acted on the same principle in Spain, the defeat he suffered at Baylen would not have tarnished the luster of his early fame, nor rested as a spot on the military glory of France. But he failed of fully apprehending the perils of his position—was enveloped between two armies, and ingloriously defeated. And you, young man, unless you view life as it is, unless you substitute the sober lessons of experience for the brilliant fancies of imagination, will find your Baylen, where you will lie, crest-fallen and crushed, between the vices of your own nature and the evil influences of vicious society.

Up, then, with a heroic spirit, and gird yourself

for mortal conflict with the great Apollyon who bestrides your pathway! If he has subdued thousands, thousands have also subdued him. And you, too, may be his conqueror. Look courageously at the chart of your intended voyage. If, by every sunken rock and beneath every dashing wave, there lies the wreck of youth who perished untimely, there is also a haven, beyond the sea, into which "*a thousand times ten thousand and thousands of thousands*" have triumphantly entered in defiance of stormy winds and roaring waves. You may do the same, if you will take timely heed to your ways. Success is before you, if you resolutely and wisely seek it. As says a modern writer, "The seas of human life are wide. Wisdom may suggest the voyage; but it must first look to the condition of the ship, and the nature of the merchandise to exchange. Not every vessel that sails from Tarshish will bring back the gold of Ophir. But shall it, therefore, rot in the harbor? No! Give its sails to the wind!"

And so say I. Yield your young heart up cheerfully to the battle of life. Calculate upon diffi-

culty; but calculate also upon success; only be
sure you do it wisely. To aid you in this task,
and to point out the safe road to eminence on
earth and to glory in heaven, is the object of the
succeeding chapters. Follow my counsels, and in
your old age you will be like the trees in Alcinou's
garden, which were covered with blossoms and
laden with fruit at the same time; in eternity, you
will flourish as a choice plant in the garden of
God.

CHAPTER II.

THE CORNER-STONE OF A SUCCESSFUL LIFE.

RICH man once undertook to erect a magnificent mansion. With free and lavish expenditure, he raised its walls, and adorned it, within and without, to suit his taste. When finished it was a stately and majestic pile of architecture. But, before it was ready for occupation, large apertures became visible in the walls. The floors and ceilings began to sink, and it was pronounced unsafe for habitation. The unwise owner had been in such unpardonable haste, as to neglect proper precautions in laying the foundation. He had built that massive structure upon an unsound surface, instead of digging down deep into the ground after the solid rock. There was no remedy but to take it all down and begin anew. This he was unable to do, having already exhausted a large proportion of his entire fortune in its construction. He was obliged, therefore, to leave it to decay and ruin—to mourn at leisure over the irreparable folly he was too hasty and too thoughtless to avoid at the beginning.

I want the young man to give this, my simple parable, an application to his own life, since he is and must be engaged in the construction of a character for two worlds. His actions and motives are to compose its materials. These, as they accumulate, will give it form and subsistence. It will be good or evil, a shelter or a curse, according to their quality. Composed of evangelically-virtuous and noble acts, it will afford quiet, honor, and comfort in this life, and, in the life to come, an abode with the blessed. Composed of unprincipled and irreligious conduct, it will yield him unrest, shame, disgrace in this world, and eternal infamy in the next.

How vastly important, then, for a young man to lay a foundation suited to the structure he designs to erect! It would be the apex of folly to think of placing a virtuous superstructure upon a substructure of vice. I apprehend no sensible young man deliberately resolves to build a bad character. Yet many, who designed to be *right* in the end, begin by indulging in follies which they intend to repudiate at length. This is building on the sand; for whether they are aware of it or not, the structure is beginning to rise, and every day's actions add to its dimensions. Nevertheless, the foundation is unsound.

Other young men, who avoid these indulgences, and pride themselves on a spotless morality, are, notwithstanding all this, also building their characters on the sand. Why are they moral? Because they wish to be respectable. Why do they refrain from the wine-cup, the card-table, the theater, the house of "*her whose feet take hold of death?*" Because they are *too proud* to be vicious. Why are they diligent, studious, careful of their reputation? Because they are ambitious of success in life. But what stability or solidity is there in pride or in ambition? Alas! they are but as the sand! The first rushing flood of tempting circumstances may wash them, and the character that stands upon them, to utter destruction!

What, then, is the true foundation of character? Where is that SOLID ROCK which will afford a firm resting-place for a virtuous life — a sure support for the noblest and most exalted character?

To this question, so big with importance to every young man, I answer, in the notable language of St. Paul, "OTHER FOUNDATION *can no man lay than that is laid*, WHICH IS JESUS CHRIST;" which means that the corner-stone of every thing truly noble in human character, of every thing really great and honorable in human life, is a saving faith in Jesus Christ. Without this, his earthly well-being is a "dread uncertainty;" the "blackness of darkness" encircles his grave, and clouds his prospect of immortality. But with it, true to the teachings of the divine Redeemer, he may be sure of rising to at least a tolerable degree of social eminence, to moderate plenty, to honor and immortal life.

The *temporal* advantages of an early religious life are not sufficiently considered by most young men. They blindly conclude that success in this life is the exclusive heritage of the worldling; that devotion to God is the surrender of present advantages and the price of eternal salvation. Never was any supposition more false. It is contrary to both experience and Scripture. True, in the infancy of Christ's religion, and in seasons of persecution, the martyred confessor mounted his triumphal chariot, from the flames of his pyre, and won his crown of life by sacrificing all terrestrial things. But you, young man, live in a land whose institutions are molded, and whose inhabitants are influenced, to a great extent, by the teachings of Jesus.

Hence, you may safely calculate upon realizing the apostolic maxim, that "*godliness is profitable* FOR ALL THINGS, *having the promise of the* LIFE THAT NOW IS, *and of that which is to come.*" You may reasonably expect that, if "*you seek first the kingdom of God and his righteousness, all these* [worldly] *things shall be added unto you.*"

The benefits of a pious life are beautifully exhibited in the third chapter of Proverbs. There religion is strikingly personified as a lovely woman standing at the portals of life's great highway, and greeting each joyous youth, as he enters, with charming words and alluring gifts. As he eagerly inquires after happiness, she exclaims, "*Happy is the man that findeth wisdom,* [religion,] *and the man that getteth understanding.*"

But the youth sees the glitter of gold, the sparkling of jewels, and the profits of merchandise, in tempting heaps, before him. His heart swells with nameless desires after the as yet unknown pleasures of sense, and he hesitates to submit to his beautiful teacher. To decide his unsettled mind, she adds: "*The merchandise of it* [religion] *is better than the merchandise of silver, and the gain thereof than fine gold. She is more precious than rubies; and* ALL THE THINGS THOU CANST DESIRE *are not to be compared unto her.*"

This is promising much; but the eye of the youth lingers still on the sensuous and gaudy offerings of sense and mammon. His charmer, therefore, proceeds to say, "*Length of days is in her right hand, and in her left hand,* RICHES AND HONOR. *Her ways are ways of pleasantness, and all her paths are peace.*"

Here are included, health, long life, prosperity, eminence among men, tranquillity, and quietude of conscience, as the results of beginning life aright; and, as if to meet the last wish of the most aspiring soul, she crowns this pyramid of blessings with a wreath from paradise, exclaiming that "she is a tree of life to them that lay hold upon her;" by which is implied that the blessed gifts of religion, in this world, are to be succeeded by a life of unending glory in the next. Could more than this be offered? Nay, there is nothing left to be desired. Only surrender your heart to the sway of piety—approach your Creator, and entreat him to bind you to religion, with the soft bands of that love which "many waters can not quench"—and you may view this world with that confidence which cries, "*The Lord is my Shepherd; I shall not want;*" and the next, with that hope which triumphantly exclaims, "*If the earthly house of this tabernacle be dissolved, we have a building, not made with hands, eternal, and in the heavens*"

I do not affirm that a religious life is the *only* road to temporal prosperity and social superiority.

Riches, honor, power, and long life, are often
gained by men who are "an abomination in the
sight of God." Superior genius will, of itself,
win popular admiration, and command civic or political honors. Brilliant business talents will make
their possessor a desirable and prosperous man. A
strong physical constitution is favorable to longev-
ity. And even duplicity, knavery, or overreaching
in trade, may fill a man's coffers with unholy gain.
Often, indeed, do the morally vile, the enemies of
Christ, climb to the high places of earth. But
their gain is their *portion*. Their advantage is
apparent, and not real. Beneath a gay and attractive exterior, they carry a sad and heavy heart.
To real contentment, to inward tranquillity, to
genuine happiness, every godless man is an utter
stranger, however high or brilliant may be his
worldly position. What irreligious worldling, however proud his success, ever, in a candid moment,
made a profession of happiness since the days of
Cain? Not one! On the other hand, multitudes
of the world's most honored and applauded heroes
have groaned forth the lamentable cry, "Our mis-

ery is greater than we can endure!" amidst pro-
fusions of honors, riches, offices, and plaudits.
Kings, princes, senators, philosophers, merchants,
warriors, and orators, without number, when at
the hight of their ambition, have signed the dec-
laration of that wise monarch, who said of this
world, "*Vanity of vanities, all is vanity!*" Let
me show you the hearts of some of these, as they
are revealed in their own recorded confessions.

VOLTAIRE, one of the most brilliant of the sons
of genius, whose friendship was courted by powerful kings, and whom the people delighted to honor,
speaking of life, said, "Life is thickly sown with
thorns; and I know of no other remedy than to
pass quickly through them."

LORD CHESTERFIELD, a British nobleman, a man
who made pleasure his chief pursuit, rich in titles,
lands, wit, learning, and opportunity, after com-
paring life to a dull, tasteless, and insipid journey,
said, "As for myself, my course is already more
than half passed over, and I mean to sleep in the
coach the rest of the journey."

BYRON, that highly-gifted but deeply-sinning

child of the Muses, describes human life in the
following sorrowful lines:

> " Alas! it is delusion all;
>   The future cheats us from afar,
> Nor can we be what we recall,
>   Nor dare we think on what we are."

To these melancholy confessions we might add
those of Nelson, Talleyrand, Randolph, and a host
beside, who, in similar language, have given une-
quivocal testimony to the absolute impossibility of
combining genuine enjoyment with a merely-worldly
life. And where is the young man who can envy
the literary glory of Voltaire, the fashionable pre-
eminence of Chesterfield, or the blazing luster of
Byron's genius, while he beholds the first so tor
tured with the thorns of life, the second so horri-
fied with its ennui, the third so tormented with
remorse and fear, that a hasty flight, a blind forgetfulness, or a reckless leap into the great deep
of consequences, is their highest consolation?
Alas! how pitiful, how inexpressibly mournful, the
sight, to see minds immortal so tormented, and so
hopelessly wretched!

How beautiful is the contrast between the gloom of these brilliant worldlings and the lofty cheerfulness of the great Christian apostle! He ranked not, like them, with the lordly, the great, the royal; but was accounted as *"the filth and offscouring of all things."* His persecutions and sufferings rained on his head, and raged around his steps in incomparable fury. Yet there he stood, firmly and calmly, amidst the foaming of the storm, his feet resting on the solid rock of Christ's promise, his eyes fastened on the love and mercy of God, which, brighter and lovelier than the rainbow, spanned the heavens; his heart beating with the glad pulsations of immortal life, and his tongue giving utterance to the sublime language of confidence, exclaiming, *"Our light affliction, which is but for a moment, worketh for us a far more exceeding and eternal weight of glory!"* Tell me, young man, if this noble bearing, this divine triumph, under the sorest of present ills, is not of more value than all the pleasures of sense, the pomp of power, or the luxuries of wealth! How infinitely preferable, therefore, must be a life consecrated to religion, in its prime, to a life of even profitable sin! To every *innocent* gratification that earth can give to the senses, religion joins a sweet repose of spirit, which must be ever unknown to those whose souls are not in harmony with their Creator. For, as the ABBE MENNAIS has beautifully said, "While a sinful life engenders suffering, and a sorrow is always hidden at the bottom of a forbidden joy, calmness, on the contrary, serenity, unvarying contentment, are the lot of a pure conscience. It resembles the sparrow, sweetly reposing in its nest, while the tempest abroad bends and breaks the tops of the forest."

Who has not heard of those triumphs of art and labor, by which the waters of the Croton and of Cochituate lake are made to flow, in iron arteries, through the streets, and into the very chambers of the citizens of two great American cities? Let us suppose that these waters, by some mysterious change, become insipid and even poisonous. Confusion, disappointment, and even intense suffering, are the immediate results. Amidst the universal dismay of such a misfortune, two men appear before the city councils, with specifics for the healing of the waters.

"I," affirms the first, "have a powder, a pinch of which will heal a gallon of the water, and render it sweet as before."

The city fathers look joyfully at each other. Water is brought. The powder is infused with eager haste; each official sips a drop or two, and pronounces it delicious. The powder is equal to the claims of the inventor. Eulogy is exhausted in its praise. They inquire the price of this great discovery; and are about to conclude a contract for its purchase, when the second man steps up, saying,

"Gentlemen, I have a specific, which, cast into the springs of the lake or the river, will heal the whole forever."

The city fathers are incredulous at first. But the man is earnest and evidently sincere. He demands a bond for an immense price, to be paid if he fulfills his promise. Otherwise, he asks nothing. Now, if these city fathers were wise, with

which of these men, think you, they would conclude a contract? Judge for them, young man,
if they ought not, at almost any cost, to purchase
the specific which would entirely remove the evil
at once.

Need I make an application of this illustration?
Can you not already perceive its force, and feel its
bearing on yourself? Know you not that the
heart, originally pure as the springs of Paradise,
has become radically unclean? that its natural
streams flow forth in bitterness exceeding the taste
of aloes, and in pollution more vile than the spumy
waves of a turbid sea? Hence, it follows that life
becomes a "heritage of woe." To escape from
this woe, every young immortal looks out of himself for help. Before him stands the genius of
this world, inviting to the "*lust of the flesh, the
lust of the eyes, and to the pride of life.*" There,
also, is the radiant form of Religion, inviting him
to the cross of Christ, to virtue, and to heaven.
The former dares not promise more than occasional
hours of delight, and makes no pretense to heal
the springs of misery, which are ever sending

their streams of sorrow through the life. The latter, like Elisha standing with his cruse of salt at the waters of Jericho, boldly promises to heal those springs, and to convert the heart into a living fountain of tranquil joy, capable of yielding sweet satisfaction under every variety of outward circumstance.

Say, then, young man, which is the choice of wisdom? As a mere question of advantage during the present life, ought you not to lay a foundation of evangelical piety? I appeal to the tribunal of your reason. I demand the verdict of your intellect. To enforce that, I implore the authority of your conscience. With your reason and conscience on the side of religion, I beg you to yield a submissive will. And, hearken! A higher voice than mine supports this appeal. From Him whom the *"heaven of heavens can not contain,"* a sound, *"still, small,"* but thrilling, steals into every young man's heart, saying, "WILT THOU NOT, FROM THIS TIME, CRY UNTO ME, MY FATHER, THOU ART THE GUIDE OF MY YOUTH!"

Take heed how you despise this appeal of your

Creator. Look at your life in its relations to him and to eternity. Contemplate your destinies from that "hight which no duration limits; where Hope spreads in immensity her indefatigable wings; where you can feel within yourself a secret force, which bears you above all time, as a light body rises from the depths of the sea. From this hight look into this narrow valley, where the first term of your existence is to be accomplished." And thus, with both worlds before you, come to the great decision to lay your foundation surely and steadfastly on Him who is the "Rock of Ages."

To be successful in life, to rise above the common herd of mankind, a young man requires certain elements of character; all of which are attainable through the power of religion, and many of which most young men never will attain without that power. He must possess INTEGRITY, that he may win public confidence; INTELLIGENCE, that he may command respect; INDUSTRY, that he may collect honey from the flowers of trade; ECONOMY and frugality, to preserve his gains; ENERGY, by which to surmount obstacles; and TACT, to enable him to adapt himself to the openings of Providence, and to make him the man for the hour of opportunity. These qualifications are, to success in life, as foundations of jasper to a royal palace. Whoever possesses them can not be an inferior man. To that man who retains them, life can not be a failure. Nay, he must rise to social superiority; he must win a commanding influence. And, hear me, young man! These elements of success are all attainable, in a greater or less degree, by every youth who will cordially embrace, and faithfully adhere to, the religion of Christ; as I will endeavor to prove, in the succeeding chapters.

CHAPTER III.

INTEGRITY NECESSARY TO SUCCESS IN LIFE.

INTEGRITY signifies incorruptibility, sound-
ness of heart, uprightness. A man of integrity is always loyal to his sense of right. His
adhesion to the principles of rectitude is so strong,
that nothing can break it. No motive is sufficiently powerful to move him from the straight
line of duty. Money can not purchase his consent
to a wrong action. Pleasure can not entice him
from the ways of justice. The pleadings of love,
the yearnings of friendship, the threatenings of
enmity, are alike powerless to move his steady soul
from its purpose to abide faithful to its convic-
tions. To the wicked in high places, who would
flatter him to turn aside from truth, for the sake
of their favor, he indignantly responds, "Shall I
sell my principles for human praise? for that

> ' Wild wreath of air—
> *That* flake of rainbow, flying on the highest
> Foam of men's deeds?' "

Ever true to his principles, his *actions* and his *duties* are as

> " Consonant cords that shiver to one note."

If duty calls him to rise up singly in defense of truth, like Noah, preaching to a world of sinners, he stands, in the noblest sublimity of moral character,

> " Like a Druid rock,
> Or like a spire of land, that stands apart,
> Cleft from the main."

If exposed to the wrath and violence of ungodly men; if the enemies of right raise threatening tempests about his head; if they pour forth floods of enmity to wash him from his high moral position, he remains unmoved and unawed at his chosen post:

> " Standing like a stately pine,
> Set in a cataract on an island crag,
> When storm is on the hights, and right and left,
> Sucked from the dark heart of the long hills, roll
> The torrents dashed to the vale."

The reply of Kossuth, the renowned hero of Hungary, furnishes a beautiful illustration of this virtue. He had escaped the pursuit of the triumphant Cossacks, and sought protection at the hands of the Sultan of Turkey. Safety, wealth, military command, were cheerfully offered to him by the Sultan, provided he would renounce the Christian religion, and embrace the doctrines of Moham'med. To refuse this condition would, for aught he knew to the contrary, be equivalent to throwing himself upon the sword of Russia, which was whetted for his destruction. But, with death frowning in his face, the heroic Kossuth nobly exclaimed, "Welcome, if need be, the ax or the gibbet; but curses on the tongue that dares to make to me so infamous a proposal!"

In this fact you see both the nature and the moral sublimity of integrity. The soul of Kossuth, long trained to a love of truth and right, revolted, with indignation, from the bare idea of purchasing his life by the sacrifice of his conscience. To die loyal to his sense of duty, however cruel the mode of his death, he regarded as infinitely preferable to life, honors, and wealth, with a violated conscience. This is integrity.

An equally-striking example is furnished, in the conduct of Ulric Zwingle, the illustrious master-spirit of the Swiss Reformation. The Pope had given Zwingle a small pension, and his legate was endeavoring to combat certain scruples which the nascent reformer indulged on the question of retaining it. The spirit of reform was beginning to stir within him, and a dim presentiment of his ultimate duty to attack the Papacy was slowly rising in his soul. Hence, he wished to be released from all ties which would hinder the freedom of his great mind. But the Papal legate insisted, and Zwingle consented to retain it awhile longer, but added these notable words:

"Do not think that for any money I will suppress a single syllable of the truth."

Noble Zwingle! Glorious loyalty to the sense of duty which not all the wealth of the Vatican can induce to surrender even a *syllable of truth!* Young man, this, too, is integrity.

At the risk of being too profuse in my illustrations of this point, I will introduce yet another and, perhaps, more striking exhibition of this essential virtue. The interest of the circumstances, and the hope that the moral beauty they disclose may strengthen the young man's allegiance to right, shall be my apology.

The Government of Scotland had, for generations, claimed a jurisdiction over the pulpits of the Scottish Church, which the latter could not conscientiously yield. A recent enforcement of this ancient claim, in a particular church, followed by abortive efforts to secure a reform, led several of its most celebrated ministers to a determination to quit the assembly, resign their churches, and organize a free Church, independent of all state control. The execution of this purpose involved the sacrifice of their livings, manses, and means of support. It would leave many of them poor, houseless, and dependent on the providence of God alone for support. The adherents of the state sneered at this resolve, and said there was no fear that many of them would make such a sacrifice for a mere scruple of conscience. The 18th of May, 1843, however, proved to Scotland and the world that the spirit of the ancient Scottish Covenanter

yet lived in the heart of her modern sons. Let
us view the scene as it transpired on that memo-
rable day, in the city of Edinburgh.

The gray old towers of Holyrood are alive with
the bustle and grandeur of reflected royalty. The
narrow streets are crowded with dense masses,
through which the gorgeous procession of the
queen's commissioner can scarcely force its way to
the cathedral church of St. Giles. The levee and
sermon past, the royal commissioner proceeds to
St. Andrew's, to meet the General Assembly.
Amidst the anxious beatings of many hearts, the
house is called to order.

Prayer is next offered, and is followed by a
brief, deep silence. Then the polished and classic
Welsh, who is moderator, "his pure and glowing
spirit shining through his fragile body, like a lamp
through a vase of alabaster," rises to his feet.
With a firm, unfaltering voice, he utters a noble
protest against the proceedings of the state. Then
laying his protest on the table, and bowing to the
commissioner, he walks toward the eastern door.
This movement raises the interest of the assembly

to its highest pitch; for who could say how many would abide true to principle and right in that stern hour of trial? Who will follow the dauntless Welsh? First, the white-haired Chalmers, with his "massive frame and lion port, springs to his side." Another and another of Scotland's most distinguished clergy follow him, till 'the pride and flower of the Church swell the gathering stream. As they pour out of the church, "a long-drawn, sobbing sigh, a suppressed cheer of admiration and sympathy, sweeps round the church," from the spectators, who gaze in solemn wonder at the sight. Dismay and astonishment mark the countenances of the royal commissioner and the adherents of the crown.

Outside of the church the excitement is still more intense. Vast masses have waited there for hours, to see if the spirit of the old Covenanter yet lived in Scotland. "When will they come?" has been asked a thousand times.

"They will *not* come!" has been as often answered back by those who had no faith in the power of principle.

4

"They *will* come!" has been the response of the old Covenanter soul.

At length a door opens; a cry of "Here they come!" announces to the multitude, and to the world, that the Evangelical Church of Scotland is free. Instantly the whole mass of people is in motion. Hats and handkerchiefs are waved aloft, and "a shout, not loud, but deep and earnest—a shout, the voice of the heart rather than of the lip—bursts from the countless thousands" who throng street, door, window, and even house-top. The long agony is over. The Church is safe. Strong men, who had faced the roar of battle unmoved, are unstrung, and the big tears gush from their eyes as they murmur, "Thank God, Scotland is free!" "Four hundred of Scotland's best ministers, and as many elders, march through that yielding crowd to Tanfield Hall, which is crowded to the roof by eager spectators. There the tremulous voice of Welsh leads in prayer, and the long-pent-up feelings of the assembly burst forth in irrepressible sobs, and tears of mingled sorrow and gladness. Then that multitude stands up, and from "four thousand voices there ascend the high and mournful strains of the old Hebrew faith and fearlessness."

> "God is our refuge and our strength,
>   In straits a present aid;
> Therefore, although the earth remove,
>   We will not be afraid."

The towers of the Cannon mills shake with the thunders of their melody; and every heart is nerved with holy fervor to lay down all for the cross and crown of Christ.*

The moral grandeur of this scene is, at least, equal to any recorded facts in the history of man. It exhibits the moral beauty of integrity. The scene owes all its sublimity to the fact that those heroic ministers were sufficiently loyal to their sense of right and duty to prefer the loss of all things to its violation. And, young man, this is the integrity I wish you to attain, as a prime element of success in life.

One of the first effects of integrity is to secure

---

* See Hetherington's History of the Church of Scotland.

to its possessor the *confidence* of society. To have
the confidence of others is to have influence over
them; for men readily yield themselves to the
guidance of those in whom they confide. Hence,
a reputation for lofty integrity is better capital than
gold; it is more persuasive than eloquence; it is
more powerful than the sword. A remarkable example of its influence is furnished in the rivalry
of Robespierre and Mirabeau, during the first
epochs of the French Revolution.

No two men, perhaps, ever presented greater
contrasts of person, ability, and character than
these politicians. Mirabeau was of patrician blood;
Robespierre an obscure plebeian. Mirabeau had
the eye of an eagle, the port of a lion, the energy
of a whirlwind, a voice of thunder, an eloquence
which stirred men's souls, commanded the assent
of his friends, and terrified his adversaries. Robespierre's eyes flashed no fire, his manner was feeble
and uncouth, his voice weak and broken, his oratory was contemptible and usually passionless. Between such men, one would think, there could be
no rivalry; for how could Robespierre, vain as he

was, dare to compete for influence with Mirabeau? But he did dare; and that, too, with success, as will appear by the following scene, which took place in the celebrated Revolutionary Club of the Jacobins, where hitherto Mirabeau had reigned supreme.

Robespierre was speaking, one night, in the Club, against a decree, which, through Mirabeau's influence, had that day passed the National Assembly. Though cold and passionless in his manner, he, nevertheless, brought such severe logic to bear against the principles of the decree, that the club greeted him with thunders of applause. Mirabeau is alarmed. He sits uneasy in his presidential chair, and at length calls Robespierre to order, saying, "No one must speak against a decree already passed by the Assembly!"

This the Club will not endure. Loud shouts for Robespierre to proceed resound through the hall. Mirabeau mounts his chair, and affirming that the attack on the decree was intended to cover an assault upon himself, appeals to his friends, crying, "Help, colleagues! let all my friends surround me."

This was manifestly an appeal to his influence over the Club. A few months before, it would have brought a rampart of some six hundred human breasts around him. But that night only *thirty* responded to his call. It was obvious that his influence had passed over to Robespierre.

What was the secret of this change? Let the young man note it carefully. Mirabeau had accepted royal gold; his political integrity had become suspected; and all his high qualifications were growing impotent. Robespierre — cold, selfish, calculating, repulsive as he was — had contrived to acquire a reputation for incorruptibility. Men believed that no price could purchase his allegiance to republican principles. Hence, they freely surrendered themselves up to his influence, till they placed him at the head of that fearful and barbarous revolution, proving that, even among unprincipled men, there is a respect for integrity which molds and leads them.

Let me exhort you, therefore, young man, to cultivate the loftiest integrity, even in connection with the smallest matters. Are you a clerk? See to it that your minutest entries are strictly correct; that you never appropriate one cent of your employer's money or property to your own uses. Deal with honorable exactness toward all who trade at your store or counting-room. Eschew all *business lies*, in selling goods. If, in measuring or weighing an article, you discern defects which lessen its value, boldly make them known. Do not permit a dishonest employer to compel you to be his instrument — his tool for doing wrong. Let him distinctly understand that *you* do not hesitate between dishonor and dismissal. Prove, if need be, by the loss of your situation, that you prefer an honest crust to a dishonest banquet. If you are a mechanic, a farmer, or an artist, prosecute your daily tasks with the same careful diligence in the absence as in the presence of your employer; thus proving that you are "*no eye-servant*," no mere "*man-pleaser*," but a conscientious and dignified young man; doing right, not for reputation's sake, but because you love it, and from a sense of obligation to almighty God.

It is by *small things* that you are to acquire a

habit of integrity. The disposition of mankind is to despise the little incidents of every-day life. This is a lamentable mistake, since nothing in this life is really small. Every event is "great, for good or for evil; because of the unfathomable mysteries that lie shrouded in the growth on earth of an immortal soul." It is only by exercising your principles in the daily tests of ordinary life that you can acquire power to stand in an extraordinary and truly-difficult position. It was only by habitual fidelity to his sense of duty that Luther or Zwingle acquired strength to withstand the flattering solicitations of the Pope. None but a mind trained, through daily tests, to an instinctive choice of right, could, like Kossuth, so promptly and unhesitatingly accept the gibbet or ax as the price of integrity. Any other mind would have paused, hesitated, employed mental casuistry, and looked, at least, after some excuse for yielding a principle and saving life. But Kossuth's mind settled the question as soon as it was stated; and thus showed itself loyal, from long habit, to virtue and to truth. Be faithful, therefore, in that which is least; thereby acquiring the power to be faithful in that which is great, should you ever be called to such a trial of your principles.

Let us enter yonder counting-room. A clerk is busy at the writing-desk. The merchant sits conversing at the table with a brother merchant. The porter calls the clerk from the counting-room. As the door closes, the visiting merchant inquires of his friend,

"Is that your chief clerk, Mr. Grey?"

"Yes, sir. He is at the head of my establishment," replies the merchant.

"Indeed! Are you not afraid to intrust so young a man with so high a responsibility?"

Mr. Grey smiles, and answers:

"No, sir. That young man has my most implicit confidence. He has been with me from his boyhood. I have never known him to betray a single trust. He identifies his interests with mine. He abhors the idea of mercantile dishonesty in every aspect; and I would intrust him with uncounted gold."

"You are fortunate to have such a clerk. De-

pend upon it, there are few such in our city,"
replies the merchant's friend, as, deeply musing,
he retires from the counting-room. The conversation has strongly impressed his mind. He conducts an extensive business; and, being somewhat
advanced in life, is desirous of finding a young
partner. The high commendation of Mr. Grey's
clerk has fixed his attention. He resolves to observe him, and, at a suitable opportunity, if satisfied, secure his services. The result is, that the
young clerk becomes first his partner, and then
the owner of the business; thus securing profit
and advancement as the reward of his integrity.

Now, I do not say that every young man of
sound principles will be equally fortunate, because
capacity, address, and other elements, must be
combined, to insure such marked and signal elevation. Yet I do not hesitate to affirm that every
young man who resembles that clerk in his uprightness of character may be sure of rising to a loftier
hight in his profession, and to more enduring fortune, than if his principles are loose, and his fidelity open to suspicion.

In some of the European states scientific men have recommended the insertion of lightning-rods in quarries, for the purpose of attracting the electric fluid during a thunder-storm, and thereby blasting the rock. The relation of those rods to the splitting of a stone fitly illustrates the influence of dishonesty, trickery in trade, or overreaching in any form, upon the fame and fortune of the clerk or merchant who condescends to its practice. Every such violation of the laws of right serves as a conductor to the retributive providences of the Creator, which, sooner or later, shiver the fabric built up by fraud into fragments. The late Gideon Lee, a celebrated American merchant, and an honest man, was accustomed to remark, that though "a man may gain a temporary advantage by selling an article for more than it is worth, yet the effect must recoil upon himself in the shape of bad debts and increased risk." The following fact, in his history, is given to illustrate his opinion:

A merchant boasted, one day, in Mr. Lee's office, of having gained a great advantage over a neighbor; and then, with the utmost barefacedness, added, "To-day I have obtained an advantage over you, too, Mr. Lee."

"Well," replied the honest man, "that may be; but if you will promise never to enter my office again, I will give you that bundle of goat-skins."

The unprincipled trader was so devoid of all self-respect, that he made the promise, took the skins, and for fifteen years did not cross Mr. Lee's threshold. At the expiration of that period, however, he walked into his office. Mr. Lee instantly recognized him, and said, "You have violated your word; pay me for the goat-skins!"

"O," replied the man, in sorrowful tones, "I have been very unfortunate since I saw you, and am quite poor!"

"Yes," said the man of probity; "and you will always be so; that miserable desire to overreach others must keep you so."*

Thus you may see that the providence of God has joined ultimate adversity to all violations of

---

* Quoted in Hunt's Merchants' Magazine.

the law of justice, just as he has united honor and
well-being with integrity. The motive, therefore,
is twofold—one of fear and another of attraction.
Honor, advancement, well-being, with their rich
emoluments, stand inviting you to the ways of
right; while disgrace, debasement, and ruin stand
frowning in the paths of deceit and dishonesty.
God himself speaks to you, saying: "*The house
of the.wicked shall be overthrown ; but the tabernacle
of the* UPRIGHT *shall flourish.*"

You are, doubtless, convinced of the beauty, the
benefit, the desirableness, of this vital element of
genuine success in life. Perhaps you have inwardly resolved to cultivate it. Animated by the
examples, pleased with the beauty, attracted by the
benefits of integrity, you have already said, in
your heart, "I will diligently cultivate this sublime virtue. With Kossuth, Zwingle, and those
noble Scotsmen, I will hold my integrity dearer
than money, honor, or life."

This is a noble resolve; but how will you keep
it ? Whence, amid the contagion of evil example,
tne lure of the apparent rewards of deceit, and the

insatiable desires of your own fiery heart, which
will soon be as eager, in the strife for fame and
fortune, as Hotspur in the battle-field, whence will
you gain strength to resist all these temptations?
By what aids do you intend to remain conqueror on
a field where millions have fallen? Consider well
the question of Jesus, who asks, " *What king,
going to make war against another king, sitteth not
down first and consulteth whether he be able with ten
thousand, to meet him that cometh against him with
twenty thousand?*" So you, counting the difficulties surrounding a young combatant after an upright reputation, should seriously ask, "Have I
strength to overcome these obstacles?"

Now, I will not deny the obvious fact, that a few
persons have won a high mercantile reputation
without the aid of experimental religion. Pride
of birth, of character, of education, a strong instinctive admiration of mercantile justice, freedom
from the pressure of strong solicitation, with other
causes, may have sustained them under their circumstances; but I contend that no young man can
rationally hope to pass the ordeals of life in safety,

unless his outward virtues derive vitality and vigor from an inward religious life. To be perennial, the stream must proceed from a living spring; to be fruitful, the tree must spread its roots in a congenial soil: so, to insure the possession of uprightness through the manifold trials of human life, the soul of a man must be in harmony with its Creator—through faith in Him, it must derive strength to resist wrong, to desire and to will right, when standing in the plunging torrent of evil influences which is ever dashing down the highways of trade. Greatly-good men are always "like solitary towers in the city of God; and secret passages, running deep beneath external nature, give their thoughts intercourse with higher intelligences, which strengthens and controls them;" and this secret intercourse with God is necessary for you, if to be greatly good is your aim and purpose.

Religion never fails to make its possessor a man of integrity. Its primary idea is a surrender of the man, soul and body, to God and to his teachings. A deliberate casting off of any one moral principle, known to be a Divine precept, is an act of apostasy from religion. It is a disavowal of the previous act of surrender, a violation of the sacred covenant. Hence, religion and integrity are as inseparable as a cause and its sequence. To embrace the former is, of necessity, to secure the latter. To yield fully to the indwelling Spirit, who chooses the religious heart for his temple, is to be in a state where the loftiest and sublimest integrity is "spontaneous and inevitable, the outward blossoming and fruitfulness of a heavenly life. It is like the skylark's hymn, the violet's fragrance, the breath of the sweet south, the morning star's sweet effulgence. The soul obeys the desires of her divine Lord with the ineffable delight, tenderness, and constancy of the bride."*

Religion should, therefore, be your first object of pursuit, if you desire to wear the ornament of an upright character. Place yourself in the hands of Jesus Christ. Yield your spirit, as an instrument of power, to the touch of his fingers, and

---

* Rev. T. L. Harris.

suffer him to call forth its delightful harmonies. Let his power be your dependence; his grace your strength. Thus will your moral sense be keen, clear, sensitive; your moral power, equal to the most powerful tests; your integrity, of the purest character; and your success in life greatly promoted.

5

CHAPTER IV.

INTELLIGENCE AN ELEMENT OF SUCCESS IN LIFE.

I THINK it is the Germans who have a pretty legend of a gentleman for whom some enamored fairy wrought a precious talisman, which had the power to attract all persons who came near the wearer to himself. The charm wrought powerfully on the companions of the fortunate nobleman, and he was loved with wondrous affection by a large circle of admiring friends.

If such a talisman were attainable at the cost of much labor, suffering, and even of danger, many a young man would seek it with incredible industry. His imagination would be charmed by the idea. He would be ready to attempt the ascent of the Andes, or the exploration of the dreary realms of the ice king around the poles.

But when that same young man is told that, unless neutralized by moral deficiencies, *knowledge* is really a precious talisman, commanding the respect and influencing the opinions and conduct of all minds within his sphere of action, elevating its possessor to influence, to honor, and, possibly, to fortune, he turns away with apathy, perhaps with scorn. He disdains mental toil. However physically industrious he may be, he is intellectually too lazy to read, reflect, and study. Books are the objects of his fixed dislike. He would be delighted to wield a commanding influence, to make a deep mark in the world; but he is too slothful, too sensuous to prosecute the studies which, by expanding, strengthening, and developing the intellect, lead to high achievements and eminence. He prefers to waste his leisure hours in idle lounging, in frivolous amusement, in unprofitable companionships. What is the consequence? It requires no prophetic afflatus to predict that such a young man will spend his days in comparative obscurity; that on his

> " Grassy grave
> The men of future times will careless tread
> And read his name upon the sculptured stone;
> Nor will the sound, familiar to their ears,
> Recall his vanished memory."

The mind is the glory of the man. The power of the countenance to attract depends more on the thoughtfulness of the soul than upon its conformity to the laws of beauty. The utmost elegance of physical formation, the most lovely and delicately-chiseled features, unless accompanied by high intellectual expression, cease to please, after they become familiar, while "dignity robes the man who is filled with a lofty thought," notwithstanding the symmetry of his features may be imperfect, and the proportions of his form unequal; and, seeing how much of success in life often depends upon outward impressions, it is important to a young man to robe himself in the attractive dignity of thought.

Next to moral worth, no possession is so productive of real influence as a highly-cultivated intellect. Wealth, birth, and official station may and do secure to their possessors an external, superficial courtesy; but they never did and they never can command the reverence of the heart. Fear of being injured by power, and hope of being benefited by wealth, induce men to offer the incense of servility at the shrines of mammon; but it is only to the man of large and noble soul, to him who blends a cultivated mind with an upright heart, that men yield the tribute of deep and genuine respect. Mental superiority has often commanded the friendship of courts and kings. It has elevated the plebeian above the patrician. What star ever shone with purer light, or commanded more admiration, in the brilliant court of France, than the plain, republican, but cultivated, Benjamin Franklin? Who ever rose to higher influence in the political circles of proud England than Cromwell, Eldon, Burke, Canning, and Brougham? To what did they owe their vast influence but to great intellectual power, developed by slow and toilsome cultivation? Is the young man ambitious of high success in life? Does he aspire to rival great names? Then, let him diligently cultivate his intellect.

Yonder, on the calm, moonlit sea, gliding in solemn majesty over the unruffled waters, is a splendid ship. Among the dark forms upon her deck may be discerned a pale-faced boy, some six-

teen summers old. He is leaning over the bul-
warks, absorbed in a dreamy reverie. His imagination is traversing the future of his career. Filled
with the gay illusions of hope, he peoples the years
to come with images of success. He beholds himself rising from post to post in his dangerous profession, till he fancies himself the commander of a
great fleet. He wins brilliant victories; wealth,
honors, fame surround him. He is a great man.
His name is in the mouth of the world. There is
a circle of glory round his brow. Filled with the
idea, he starts. His young heart heaving with
great purposes, his eyes gleaming with the fire of
his enkindled soul, his slender form expanding to
its utmost hight, and his lips moving with energy,
he paces the silent deck, exclaiming, "I will be a
hero; and, confiding in Providence, I will brave
every danger."

Such was the romantic dream of young Horatio
Nelson, afterward the hero of the Nile, the victor
of Trafalgar, and the greatest naval commander in
the world. And what young man has not had im-
aginings equally romantic? Where is the poor

sailor-boy who has not dreamed of glory and greatness? What young law student has not seen in
himself a future Littleton, Coke, or Story? Where
is the printer's apprentice who has not intended to
be a Franklin? What young mechanic has not, in
fancy, written his name beside the names of Ark-
wright, Fulton, or Rumford? What boyish artist
has not, in imagination, rivaled Raphael or Michael
Angelo? What youthful orator has not gathered
the glory of Burke, Chatham, or Patrick Henry
around his own name? Nay. There never was a
young man of any advantages who did not rise to
eminent success, in his hours of reverie. For,
youth is the period of dreams, in which Queen
Mab, with her fairy crew, holds undisputed reign
over the imagination, and revels at will in the
hall of fancy, in the palace of the soul.

But why, since *all* dream of greatness, do so few
attain it? Why stand Nelson, Story, Fulton,
Burke, etc., alone, in the realization of their im-
aginings, among ten thousand of their peers, whose
early dreams were as bright and as vivid as their
own? Why do so few young men distinguish

themselves, out of the many whose hopes, purposes, and resolves are as radiant as the colors of the rainbow?

The answer is obvious. Young men are not willing to devote themselves to that process of slow, toilsome self-culture, which is the price of great success. Could they soar to eminence on the lazy wings of genius, the world would be filled with great men. But this can never be; for whatever aptitude for particular pursuits nature may donate to her favorite children, she conducts none but the laborious and the studious to distinction. Cicero and Demosthenes, those unrivaled orators of antiquity, were diligent students. Sir William Jones, the greatest of oriental scholars; Newton, the first of philosphers; Burke, the chief of modern orators; Michael Angelo, the model of artists; Haydn and Handel, those peerless masters of the musical art; John Quincy Adams, the diplomatist and statesman; all mounted the throne of their fame step by step. Their glory gathered around them by degrees. Each added ray was the result of intense application. It was not genius, so much as

GENIUS SEDULOUSLY CULTIVATED, that enabled them to write their names so high on the pillar of fame. Great men have ever been men of thought, as well as men of action. As the magnificent river, rolling in the pride of its mighty waters, owes its greatness to the hidden springs of the mountain nook, so does the wide-sweeping influence of distinguished men date its origin from hours of privacy, resolutely employed in efforts after self-development. The invisible spring of self-culture is the source of every great achievement.

Away, then, young man, with all dreams of superiority, unless you are determined to dig after knowledge as men search for concealed gold. If you lack the resolution, the manly strength of purpose, needed to bind you to reading, reflection, and study, you may bid adieu to all hope of marked success. Your destiny is settled. You will dwell in ignoble nothingness, far down the vale of obscurity. Your name will be "writ in water."

Yet, why need you surrender all your cherished hopes of distinction? The assured fact that the great mass of the young men of your age will spend their youth in frivolity and self-neglect, gives the individual who is determined to be a fully-developed man the greater certainty of rising above his peers. Resolve, therefore, to act a part worthy of that intellect with which God has endowed you! Dare to contend for the palm of superiority!

Success is certain, if you do your best; as says an eccentric writer, "Show me the man who has made the most of his faculties, and I will show you a being sublimated to the hight of the angelic nature." This is strongly expressed; but it nevertheless contains a great truth. Every man has in himself the seminal principle of great excellency. The reader has it, and he may develop it by cultivation, if he will TRY.

Perhaps you are what the world calls *poor* What of that? Most of the men whose names are as household words, were also the children of poverty. Captain Cook, the circumnavigator of the globe, was born in a mud-hut, and started in life as a cabin-boy. Nelson, England's greatest admiral, was only a coxswain in his youth. Lord

Eldon, who sat on the woolsack, in the British Parliament, for nearly half a century, was the son of a coal-merchant.   Franklin, the philosopher, diplomatist, and statesman, was but a poor printer's ooy, whose highest luxury, at one time, was only a penny roll, eaten in the streets of Philadelphia. Ferguson, the profound philosopher, was the son of a half-starved weaver.   Heyne, the renowned German scholiast, was born in a poor peasant's cot. Burns, the bard of Scotland, ate the coarse bread of labor.   The lamented Kirke White, the youthful poet, was the son of a butcher.   Whitefield, the most renowned of pulpit orators, was the son of a tavern-keeper.   John Wesley, the greatest ecclesiastical legislator of his age, was the son of a poor village vicar, whose scanty income scarce sustained his numerous children.   Johnson, Goldsmith, Coleridge, Keats, Crabbe, all knew the pressure of limited circumstances; yet they made themselves a name.   They, with many others, have demonstrated that limited means, or poverty even, is no insuperable obstacle to success.   Their history shows that the most stupendous difficulties

may be defied and conquered by steadily and perseveringly cultivating the mind, and thus fitting it
beforehand for the openings of Divine providence.
Poesy never sang more truly than in the following
beautiful lines of Longfellow, in his "Psalm of
Life:"

> "Lives of great men all remind us
> We can make our lives sublime,
> And, departing, leave behind us
> Footprints on the sands of time;
>
> Footprints that, perhaps, another,
> Sailing o'er life's solemn main,
> A forlorn and shipwrecked brother,
> Seeing, may take heart again."

Up, then, young man, and gird yourself for the
work of self-cultivation! Set a high price on your
leisure moments. They are sands of precious gold.
Properly expended, they will procure for you a
stock of great thoughts—thoughts that will fill,
stir, invigorate, and expand your soul. Seize also
on the unparalleled aids furnished by steam and
type, in this unequaled age. The great thoughts
of great men are now to be procured at prices
almost nominal; therefore, you can easily collect a
library of choice authors. Public lectures are also

abundant in our large cities. Attend the best of them, and carefully treasure up their richest ideas. But, above all, learn to reflect even more than you read. Reading is to the mind what eating is to the body, and reflection is similar to digestion. To eat without giving nature time to assimilate the food to herself by the slower process of digestion, is to deprive her first of health, and then of life; so, to cram the intellect by reading, without due reflection, is to weaken and paralyze the mind. He who reads thus, has "his perceptions dazzled and confused by the multitude of images presented to them; and this because he has not the faculty of pausing at every point of interest—of weighing, searching, and questioning—of arbitrating between truth and the author—of improving hints and verifying conclusions. Without thought, books are the sepulchers of the soul. They not only immure it, but, like thieves in the candle, while they obscure its light, they consume the bodily substance, and so hasten its dissolution."* But let thought and

---

* Self-formation.

reading go hand in hand, and the intellect will rapidly increase in strength and in gifts. Its possessor will rise in character, in potentiality, in positive influence. His success, his moral qualities being equal, will be assured.

But here I have reached a point of the highest importance to every young man; and that point is, the necessity of religion to give right direction to the cultivated intellect. Mental power alone is not a guarantee of innocent and virtuous superiority. A life of study gave the philosophic Bacon power and renown; but the absence of religious principle left him to disgraceful deeds, which will dim the luster of his fame forever. Men will honor his intellect, but despise his heart. So of Lord Byron, Rousseau, Voltaire, and others. Education is as a mighty steam-engine to a ship—it gives her power—skillfully regulated, it enables her to mount the loftiest wave, and wage successful war with the fiercest storm—directed by violence and hate, it makes her powerful to destroy—submitted to ignorance, it carries her to destruction on the rock, or rends her to fragments in mid air. Thus, education, controlled by rectitude, is powerful for good—swayed by depravity, it spreads destruction over society, and destroys its possessor.   Tennyson thus beautifully paints an educated mind unsanctified by the Spirit of God.   He calls it

> "A sinful soul possessed of many gifts;
> A spacious garden, full of flowering weeds;
> A glorious devil, large in heart and brain,
> That did love beauty only—beauty seen
> In all varieties of mold and mind—
> And knowledge for its beauty; or, if good,
> Only for its beauty."

Permit me to conduct you to an English village, as it appeared some two hundred years ago.   As your eye wanders among its ancient cottages, with huge gable-ends and roofs of thatched straw, let it rest upon a group of young men, surrounding one whose mean dress and bag of tools proclaim him to belong to the humble fraternity of traveling tinkers.   He is the chief speaker, and his conversation is remarkable only for its extravagant profanity. With a vulgar air, and a boisterous manner, he rolls out a filthy stream of oaths from the fountain of a deeply-polluted spirit. Suddenly, however, his vile speech is arrested by the presence of a low, forbidding creature. An old, wrinkled crone, with little, twinkling eyes, a cracked voice, and a hand resting on each hip, pushes her way through the group, and, gazing earnestly in the blasphemer's face, exclaims,

"You curse and swear at such an ungodly rate that I tremble to hear you! You are the ungodliest person for swearing I ever heard in my whole life!"

The young sinner stands amazed and stricken under this rebuke; for the reprover is herself notorious for vulgarity and cursing. Deep, big thoughts rush through his startled soul; he inwardly but sternly resolves to be a better man. That day's events form an epoch in his life. Erelong it becomes known that the swearing tinker is transformed into the exemplary Christian. Soon his voice is heard preaching Christ. Persecution breaks forth against him. The harpies of bigotry hunt him from the pulpit to the prison. For twelve years he lies confined in a miserable dungeon, whose walls are ever dripping with damp, for the notable offense of preaching the Gospel! But, from that dim apartment, he sends forth a book, whose original conception, grand and beautiful imagery, touching pathos, purity of style, and truthfulness to nature and experience, give its author an almost unrivaled fame. And to-day the tomb of John Bunyan, the converted tinker, the author of the Pilgrim's Progress, is sought out by the loftiest sons of genius, who stand upon the sweet dreamer's ashes, and sigh for the inspiration which gave enchantment to his pen.

The point, in this illustration, which it is important to the young man to notice, is, that it was religion which called the hidden powers of Bunyan's intellect into exercise, and directed them to a holy end. But for religion, instead of being a star of surpassing beauty, shedding the purest rays of soft and holy light on the human intellect, he would have lived a loathsome human reptile, crawling in the dust, and spitting the venom of death upon mankind. He would have died

"Silent, unseen, unnoticed, unlamented."

6

To religion, therefore, as the grand stimulant, the mighty developing agent of the human intellect, should every young man direct his fixed attention. A power of unknown extent resides in its great ideas. Great thoughts always stir the attentive mind, just as high winds cause the thick leaves of the tree to rustle. They enlarge it, too. The soul of a philosopher lives in a wider sphere, and experiences nobler emotions, than the soul of a peasant, only because it has become conversant with the grandeur of the universe. Let the peasant employ the same means, and his confined spirit, bursting the cerements of its intellectual sepulcher, will soar freely into realms of glorious thought. But religion brings the soul into contact with loftier and grander ideas than belong to the province of philosophy. Before the gaze of a seeker after Christ, it unfolds the sublime idea of GOD. It leads forth the awakened mind from the narrow boundaries of worldly thought into the vastness of the INFINITE, and bids it stretch its powers in the attempt to comprehend ETERNITY! It reveals to the mind the consciousness of its own immortality; to its moral perceptions it unfolds the stern grandeur of immutable justice, the tremendous results of evil, and the transcendent beauty of holiness. To soothe its fears and attract its hopes, it displays the idea of love, as manifested in the character and death of the great God-man, Jesus Christ.

It is impossible for the most stultified intellect to be brought into contact with these overwhelming thoughts, without being awakened from its slumbers and startled into action. Hence, the introduction of the Christian religion to a nation is the epoch of its mental birth; and the entrance upon a spiritual life has proved the birth-hour of a new intellectual life to thousands of individual Christians. It is the fault of its recipients that it is not so to all.

Religion also *strengthens*, as well as awakens, the intellect. Its primary condition — faith in Christ — requires the highest exercise of the powers of abstraction and attention. For faith is the trustful gaze of the soul on the face of Jesus Christ — the concentration of a sinner's mind and heart

on the idea of a sin-forgiving God. It necessarily involves the exercise of complete *abstraction* and powerful *attention*.   As this faith is
required to be habitual, its operations must
strengthen these important faculties.   Beside this,
religion leads to the study of that great book, the
Bible.   Here are found the seeds of impregnating,
healthy thought — the sublimest poetry, the purest
history, the most touching biography, and the pro-
foundest philosophy.   The study of these excellences naturally leads to that of collateral history,
and to the highest exercises of the intellect, so
that it is impossible for a' believer in Christ to be
faithful to the duties and teachings of religion,
without thereby developing his intellect, and becoming a man of power: as in the case of Bunyan — of Newton, the admired author of the Olney
hymns — of Richard Watson, the celebrated orator
and theologian — and thousands more, whose mental strength lay hidden even from themselves, till
called out by the power of divine truth.

Behold, in these statements, young man, another
argument in favor of a religious life.   Embrace

Christ as the best, perhaps the only means of bringing your intellect into a state of vigorous and healthy life—as the guardian angel of your genius, if it be already manifested. Yield yourself up honestly and fully to the claims of God in Christ. Be a spiritual, intellectual Christian. Thus shall your mental and moral powers grow in harmonious proportion. Your heart shall be warm with emotions of love; your understanding strong, mature, potential; your conscience, illuminated, quick, and pure; your *will* upright, controlling, and inflexible. These things being in you and abounding, you can hardly fail of success in the great battle of life, nor of rising to the honor of Christ's glorious kingdom in the life to come. Decide, therefore, O young man, to listen attentively to the voice of Jesus Christ. Let him woo you to himself, through the sweet lines of the sacred poet, who thus beautifully sings:

"The wild dove hath her nest;
Earth, in her bosom, shields the timid hare;
Flowers sleep 'neath heaven's azure fane; but where,
Except ye come to me, shall ye find rest?

THE YOUNG MAN'S COUNSELOR.

Ye of the troubled breast,
Weighed down with sorrow, and of life aweary,
Whose paths extend through deserts waste and dreary
    Come, then, to me; I will impart relief.

In life's glad summer come;
Earth's lovely things, the beautiful, the gay,
Are they not swept as autumn leaves away?
    So pass your hopes and visions to the tomb.

Though by the world caressed,
Though all its treasures glitter at your feet,
And life's young years with rapture be replete,
    O, what are these to heaven—a heaven of rest!"

CHAPTER V.

ENERGY AN ELEMENT OF DISTINCTION.

"IT is impossible!" said one of Napoleon's staff officers, in reply to his great commander's description of a plan for some daring enterprise.

"IMPOSSIBLE!" cried the emperor, with indignation frowning on his brow; "*impossible* is the adjective of fools!"

This may be an apocryphal anecdote of the imperial conqueror; but it is at least characteristic. It displays that consciousness of power to overcome the mightiest obstacles, and to accomplish the most extravagant purposes, which was one of the chief elements of his early success. Its language is the strong expression of a mind charged with an energy alike irresistible and unconquerable. And every young man who hopes to stand triumphant at the goal of life, must possess a measure of this energy proportionate to the exigencies of his condition.

Energy is force of character — inward power. It imports such a concentration of the will upon the realization of an idea, as enables the individual to march unawed over the most gigantic barriers, or to crush every opposing force that stands in the way of his triumph. Energy knows of nothing but success; it will not hearken to voices of discouragement; it never yields its purpose; though it may perish beneath an avalanche of difficulty, yet it dies contending for its ideal.

LONGFELLOW'S EXCELSIOR is a beautiful embodiment of the idea of energy. Its hero is a young man seeking genuine excellence; proving himself superior to the love of ease, the blandishments of passion, and the sternest outward difficulties. .The reader beholds him ascending the rugged steeps of the Upper Alps, at the dangerous hour of twilight. In his hand he bears a banner, whose strange device, "EXCELSIOR," is the visible expression of his noble purpose, to attain the hight of human excellence. His brow is sad, his eyes are gleaming with the light of lofty thought, his step is firm and elastic, while his deep, earnest cry,

'EXCELSIOR!" rings with startling effect among
the surrounding crags and glaciers.   Ease, in the
form of an enchanting cottage, with its cheerful
fireside, invites him to relax his effort.   Danger
frowns upon him from the brow of the awful avalanche, and from the "pine tree's withered branch."
Caution, in the person of an aged Alpine peasant,
shouts in his ear, and bids him beware; while
Love, in the form of a gentle maiden, with heaving breast and bewitching voice, woos him to her
quiet bowers.   But vain are the seductions of love,
the voices of fear, or the aspects of danger.   Regardless of each and of all, animated by his sublime aims, intent on success, he only grasps his
mysterious banner more firmly, and bounds with
swifter step along the dangerous steep.   Through
falling snows, along unseen paths, amidst intense
darkness, beside the most horrible chasms, he pur-
sues his way, cheering his spirit, and startling the
ear of night with his battle-cry, "Excelsior!" till,
on reaching the summit, in the moment of accomplished purpose, his work done, his manly form
chilled by the cold breath of the frost, he falls—

yea, nobly falls—into the treacherous snow-drift,
and

> "There in the twilight, cold and gray,
>   Lifeless, but beautiful, he lay;
>   And from the sky, serene and far,
>   A voice fell, like a falling star,
>   Excelsior!"

From the summit of human attainment on earth,
he had gone to dwell in the blessed heaven of God.
There his spirit, bathed in light, soars forever
amidst the unspeakable glories of the Infinite.

This is a beautiful ideal of an energetic youth
triumphing, even to the salvation of his immortal
soul. May the dream of the poet be realized in
the experience of the reader!

Energy is the soul of every great achievement;
while enervation emasculates the spirit, and dooms
the man to obscurity and ill success. Men of
feeble action are accustomed to attribute their
misfortunes to what is vulgarly termed "*ill luck*."
They envy the men who climb the ladder of eminence, and call them "the favorite children of
fortune—lucky men, and men of ·peculiar oppor-

tunity." This is a vain and foolish imagination. It is not ill fortune, so much as an enervated mind, that keeps thousands in inglorious obscurity. The blundering student, who stammers out an ill-learned lesson in his college class, and gains his diploma, at last, through indulgence rather than merit, owes his degraded position more to that voluntary mental imbecility which has ever shrunk from the labor of study, than to any absolute mental inferiority. His triumphant classmate, who quits his college adorned with the proudest honors of his Alma Mater, is as much indebted to his persevering energy, as to his native genius, for his honorable victory. He might, had he been equally supine, have been equally degraded with his unhonored classmate. But his energy saved him. So, in all the other walks of life, energy produces good fortune and success, while enervation breeds misfortune and "*bad luck.*"

If any young man desires a confirmation of these ideas, let him carefully study the history of every man who has written his name on the walls of the Temple of Fame. Let him view such minds in their *progress* toward greatness. He will see them rising step by step, in the face of stubborn difficulties, which gave way before them only because their courage would not be daunted, nor their energy wearied. He will find no exception, in the history of mankind. Supine, powerless souls have always fainted before hostile circumstances, and sank beneath their opportunities; while men of power have wrestled with sublime vigor against all opposing men and things, and obtained success because they would not be defeated.

I might illustrate these views from the biography of any eminent man; but I select CHRISTOPHER COLUMBUS as peculiarly adapted to my purpose. He was the son of an obscure wool-comber, in indigent circumstances, at Genoa. His early education was limited. Bred to the profession of seamanship, and having a strong passion for geographical studies, his thoughtful mind conceived the idea that unknown empires existed west of the great Atlantic. He dwelt upon this thought till it became fixed in his mind with singular firmness. It fired his soul with noble enthusiasm; it gave elevation to his spirit; it clothed his person with dignity, and inspired his demeanor with loftiness. Thus animated, he resolved to realize the truth of his great conception. Now came the test of his character. The idea itself was grand, and its conception bespoke the possession of a towering and glorious intellect. But, to make that conception a reality, to prove himself a true son of Genius, and not a mere romantic dreamer, required the exercise of such a measure of faith, self-reliance, and enduring energy as is seldom demanded of any man, even in the greatest of human enterprises.

But Columbus felt equal to his work, and he set about it with a purpose to do it. How sublime does he appear in his conflict with poverty, ridicule, and ignorance! The announcement of his beloved idea was greeted with torrents of derisive sarcasm, from prince and peasant, from learned savans and stupid dunces. Powerless and moneyless himself, he required the patronage of the powerful. Hence, he placed himself at the foot of the Portuguese throne, stated his views, and demanded ships to explore the ocean. Treated with fraud unworthy of a court, the intrepid man fled to Genoa, and importuned for aid in his native city. Unable to rouse the ambition of his countrymen, he repaired to Venice, and met with similar disappointment. From thence he traveled to Spain, and pleaded his cause before the lordly Ferdinand, and his great-minded queen, Isabella. There he was amused with promises of ships and men, for several years, during which time he perseveringly followed the court in its frequent journeyings. At last, wearied with their delays, but still resolute in his purpose, he prepared to quit Spain, and turned his footsteps toward the court of France. Arrested on his journey by the persuasions of an intelligent monk, he returned to Isabella's court, obtained the long-delayed means, and set sail on seas whose waters had never been cleaved by a vessel's prow.

With what high and confident expectation did the adventurous discoverer pass the boundaries of former navigation! With what patient zeal did he overcome the superstition which made cowards of his mariners, and the ignorant envy which very nearly converted them into mutineers! By the force of his own indomitable will alone, he soothed their fears, and held them to their duties, till he proudly anchored his vessels off the shores of the New World. And when the haughty flag of Spain flaunted in the breezes of the western hemisphere, as the sign of its subjugation to the crown of Isabella, it chiefly proclaimed the moral majesty of that unconquerable energy through which the noble-minded Columbus had singly defied the most formidable obstacles, and revealed a hidden world to the wondering eyes of mankind.

Are you, my reader, an aspirant after distinguished success? Then you must diligently cultivate an untiring, persisting, victorious energy, like that which gave Columbus his renown. Is your lot lowly and your sphere very limited? Are your difficulties apparently insurmountable? What then? Are you, therefore, to write yourself *a nothing*, and remain a cipher in society? Nay!

You must rather bring an irresistible force of character to bear upon every work of life. Be supine in nothing. Never despair of success in any judicious enterprise. Resolve to accomplish whatever you undertake; and though you may not discover a new world, like Columbus; nor introduce mankind to the occult mysteries of nature, like Newton; nor attain the wealth of Rothschild, or Astor; yet you may climb to the summit of your profession, attain to honorable distinction, and transmit to your posterity that most valuable of all bequests—*a good name.*

Yet you must beware of *rashness.* Successful energy is a Bucephalus, guided by the hand of an Alexander; rashness is as Mazeppa's fiery steed, unbridled and unrestrained, bearing its rider over hill and dale, to probable destruction. The former is power, guided by wisdom; the latter is power, goaded to act by blind impulses. Many men, now pining in discouragement, have expended energy sufficient for the highest success. But they have failed of their reward, because they sought not for counsel at the lips of wisdom. Rash enterprises, impetuously begun, hurried them to ruin. In their business, they resembled an oriental warrior, named DERAR, who was once sent, with a small force, by ABU BEKER, the Moslem caliph, to hinder the progress of an advancing army, near the plains of Damascus. Derar found the foe to consist of masses of troops sufficient to overwhelm his little band; but, instead of hovering round their flank, and harassing their march, he foolishly resolved on a regular attack. His voice thundered his battle-cry, and, followed by the flower of his chivalric soldiers, he rushed, with the fury of a whirlwind, upon the astonished enemy. So fiery was his onset that the foe gave way, and their rich standard fell into the hands of the bold assailant. But his success was of brief duration; numbers speedily prevailed, and Derar fell wounded into the hands of his enemies. Every Moslem in his devoted little troop would have perished, but for the timely approach of the main body of the Arab army, which arrived in season to rescue them from destruction.

Thus has many a mercantile Derar rushed madly upon an army of debts, which, after harassing him

7

into a premature old age, have led him forth, a
poor, dispirited creature, into the bondage of bankruptcy.

Beware, then, young man, of mistaking rashness for energy! They are so nearly allied that
the mistake is easy. To guard you as much as
possible, I will draw a simple sketch of a rash
man, plunging, through excess of energy—which
is the same thing with rashness—into business
ruin.

I will call him EDGAR. In his youth he was
apprenticed to a respectable tailor, became a superior workman, and, as soon as his apprenticeship
expired, determined, without capital, and contrary
to the advice of all his friends, to commence business on his own account. His reputation as a good
apprentice procured him credit. He hired a store,
purchased a small stock of goods, and rejoiced to
see his name shining in gilt letters as a merchant
tailor. Custom came in freely; success seemed
sure, notwithstanding the fears of his cautious
friends. He redoubled his efforts, increased his
stock, ornamented his store, and made quite a stir

among business men. Such were his activity,
punctuality, and industry, that his business continued to advance; and in a year or two it ex-
ceeded that of many older firms in his vicinity.
He now married, and for a time every thing went
on prosperously. But he was ambitious of having
the finest store and the largest stock of any dealer
in his line of business. Hence, he constantly purchased beyond the necessities of his business. As
a sequence, his notes matured before the means
came in, and he began to be seen in the street,
running from store to store with the question,
" Have you any thing over to-day?"

The frequency of these calls, and the difficulty
he found in promptly paying the sums thus gener-
ously loaned, awakened suspicion as to his safety,
and his fellow-merchants soon met his question
with an almost universal negative. This ought to
have checked his passion for a large stock. But,
eager as ever for display, he persisted in buying
beyond the immediate demands of his trade. As
a thrifty merchant, too, he thought he must elevate his style of living. A better house, expensive

furniture, a servant, the luxuries of the table, soon absorbed large portions of his profits. Still his notes came to maturity with alarming rapidity. Driven to extremity, he resorted to that side-door to ruin, a broker's office. Exorbitant interest only increased his embarassments. His temper grew sour; visions of ruin and bankruptcy floated before his eyes, and made him nervous and unhappy. He struggled, like a giant in bonds, for a few years; but, after growing prematurely gray in the conflict, he was forced to submit. His disgraced name appeared in the Gazette; and to-day Edgar sits on the bench, laboring for a scanty support as an unknown journeyman tailor—a discouraged man.

It is easy for the reader to see that Edgar ruined himself by excess of energy; or, in other words, by rashness. Had he taken prudent advice at the beginning, and acquired a small capital in advance; had he then wisely regulated his purchases by his actual resources, and restrained his personal expenses within the limit of his means, his strong force of character would have placed him among the first men of his class.   But he was rash, and, therefore, he was ruined.   His example is placed before the young merchant, that, as a beacon upon a sunken rock warns the mariner of danger, it may save him from a similar fate.

The energy of many men is *impulsive*.   It is to-day a dashing, roaring torrent; to-morrow it is a stagnant pool.   An accidental circumstance will call out every power of their souls, and, for a season, they will excel themselves, and startle their friends.   But they speedily spend their force, and lapse into stupid somnolency, till roused again by some bugle blast of excitement.   Such minds accomplish but little.   They lose more in their slumbers than they gain in their fitful hours of action. The calm, steady energy of the snail, slow as are its movements, is better calculated to produce results than the spasmodic leaps of the hare. Hence, in the formation of character, it is of vital importance to cultivate a steady, uniform, unyielding energy.

But how is this high qualification to be gained? Where is this precious possession to be obtained?

I know of no means so certain and effectual as that
of surrendering the soul to the claims of religion,
the direct tendency of which is to call the whole
force of the intellect and the affections into the
highest and healthiest state of action. What is
the grand central command of the Bible? *"Thou
shalt love the Lord thy God with all thy* HEART, *with
all thy* SOUL, *and with all thy* MIGHT!" Here
you see that energy of the loftiest character is
demanded of the Christian. Nor is the command
permitted to approach him as an impossible attainment; for, to every sincere creature who resolves
to submit to the commandment, the promise of
God says, *"My grace is sufficient for thee."* Thus
divine power works with the human, and the man,
in the might of his soul, stands forth as the servant of God.

Nor is it in his religious duties alone that the
Christian is required and enabled to be *energetic.*
The Scriptures demand the application of a similar
force of mind to all the duties of life. With au-
thority they thunder in the ears of the disciple,
"WHATSOEVER *thy hand findeth to do, do it with*

thy MIGHT !" Thus, whether his work be to fell a
tree, to plow a field, to build a house, to labor in
the pulpit, to plead at the bar, or to pray in the
closet, the law is, "DO IT WITH THY MIGHT!"

There is a profound meaning in this command,
rarely observed. It contains the philosophy of
growth and of greatness. It teaches that it is by
the exercise of energy, in *little* things, we are to
acquire power to triumph in great ones; that what
we find to be done, we are TO DO—not to shrink
from doing, because of its difficulty. Thus, by degrees, the soul is trained to put forth a force proportionate to its tasks; it grows in might, and con-
quers by habit. Every thing it does is well done.
It lives to subdue opposing forces. Instead of
being the sport of circumstances, it seizes them as
their master, and its career is one of perpetual
triumph.

Would you have energy, young man? Seek it
at the cross of Christ. Let the spirit of Jesus
clothe you with its divine beauty, and stimulate
you by its mighty, life-giving force. Only be true
to its holy promptings, and you will surely acquire

the energy which grapples successfully with the obstacles of this terrestrial life, and climbs to the hight of the celestial and eternal land.

CHAPTER VI.

INDUSTRY THE HIGHWAY TO SUCCESS.

I HAVE somewhere read an old legend, which, however false in fact, contains a precious lesson. It states that, some centuries ago, a man, resident in Egypt, became a convert to the Christian faith. The spirit of the times favored asceticism; and he, being of a contemplative mind, conceived the unnatural desire that if he could retire far from human society, and spend his days in solitary contemplation, he should attain to the perfection of human happiness on earth. Filled with this thought, he bade adieu to the abodes of men, wandered far into the desert, selected a cave, near which flowed a living spring, for his home, and, subsisting on the scanty crops of roots and herbs which sprang up spontaneously in the adjacent glens and valleys, began his life of meditation and prayer.

He had not spent many seasons in his hermitage before his solitary heart grew miserable beyond endurance. The long, weary hours of the day, and the dreary, interminable night, oppressed and crushed his listless soul. In the extremity of his wretchedness, he fell upon his face, and cried, "Father, call home thy child! Let me die! I am weary of life!"

Thus, stricken with grief, he fell asleep; and, in his vision, an angel stood before him, and spoke, saying, "Cut down the palm-tree that grows beside yon spring, and of its fibers construct a rope!"

The vision passed away, and the hermit awoke with a resolution to fulfill his mission. But he had no ax, and, therefore, journeyed far to procure one. On his return, he felled the tree, and diligently labored till its fibers lay at his feet, formed into a coil of rope. Again the angel stood before him, and said, "Dominic, you are now no longer weary of life, but you are happy. Know, then, that man was made for labor; and prayer also is his duty. Both are essential to his happiness. Go, therefore, into, the world, with this rope girded upon thy loins. Let it be a memorial to thee of what God expects from man!"

This beautiful legend illustrates a truth which every young man should engrave on his heart—that *industry is essential to the enjoyment of life.* It is a law of the human constitution that mankind shall find their happiness and their development in action; and it were as easy to grasp the forked lightning, or to stay the fiery waves of the volcano, as to contravene this law. Nay, it can not be; for He who said, *"In the sweat of thy face shalt thou eat bread till thou return unto the ground,"* has established this inseparable connection between industry and enjoyment.

Industry implies regular and habitual devotion to a *useful* pursuit. It is covetous of *moments,* and guards them as a miser his grains of gold. Moments, to the industrious man, are as flowers to bees—they furnish him with the opportunity of accomplishing his ends. He beholds in them the fractional parts of his life, and applies the maxim of the economist to their expenditure. His rule is, "Take care of the moments, and the years will take care of themselves." He is assiduous, not as a "hen over an addled egg," but to bring benefit out of his assiduity. He knows that it is possible to be always "busy about nothing," like Æropus, the Macedonian king, who wasted his life while busy in making lanterns! or, like Prince Bonbennin, in Goldsmith's "Citizen of the World," who was never more idle than when traversing his kingdom, searching after a "pretty white mouse with green eyes."

Behold yon graceful and sprightly "swallow, zigzagging over the clover-field, skimming the limpid lake, whisking round the steeple, or dancing gayly in the sky! Behold him in high spirits, shrieking out his ecstasy, as he has bolted a dragon-fly, or darted through the arrow-slits of an old turret, or performed some other feat of-hirundine agility! And notice how he pays his morning visits—alighting elegantly on some

house-top, and twittering politely, by turns, to
the swallow on either side of him; and. after
five minutes' conversation, off and away, to call
for his friend at the castle.   And now he is
gone upon his travels—gone to spend the winter
at Rome or Naples, to visit Egypt or the Holy
Land, or perform some more *recherche* pilgrimage
to Spain or the coast of Barbary.   And when
he comes home next April, sure enough he has
been abroad : charming climate—highly delighted
with the cicadas in Italy, and the bees on Hy-
mettus — locusts in Africa rather scarce this
season; but, upon the whole, much pleased with
his trip, and returned in high health and
spirits."

Such is the severe satire which the popular
Robert Hamilton employs to chastise that large
class of busy idlers which abounds in Europe,
and which is fast multiplying in America.   How
degraded a thing is life as thus spent by a fashionable young man of the world, whose *"chief
end"* seems to consist in puffing cigars, and in
conforming, as near as may be, to the example

of the swallow in the above picture. No wonder that, long before such young men attain meridian, they exclaim, with "CROAKER," in Goldsmith's "Good-natured Man," that "life, at the greatest and best, is but a froward child, that must be humored and coaxed a little, till it falls asleep, and then all the care is over." Shame on such young men! Beside them the twittering swallow is honorable and elevated. The bird was made for such a life, and thus fulfills its destiny; but that silly youth was made to be a MAN!—to commune with God, to labor in the holy charities and sublime duties of life.

To be industrious, then, a young man must have a *useful pursuit* and a worthy aim. He must follow that pursuit diligently. Rising early, and economizing his moments, he must earnestly persist in his toil, adding little by little to his capital stock of ideas, influence, or wealth. He must learn to glory in his labor, be it mechanical agricultural, or professional. He must impress himself deeply with the idea that a life of idleness is one of the direst of all curses. The

doctrine that labor, even of the humblest character, is dishonorable, he must resolutely trample
in the dust as false and dangerous, and contend
that an industrious, honest scavenger is really a
more honorable man than the most fashionable
dandy, who idles away his time on the pavements
of Broadway, in ladies' drawing-rooms, in cafes,
and in theaters. Thus, eschewing false ideas,
and making every moment fruitful of some good
to mind or body, to himself or to others, he can
not fail of a plenteous harvest of advantages as
life advances. *" Seest thou a man diligent in his
business? He shall stand before kings. He shall
not stand before mean men."* *" The hand of the
diligent shall rule."*

I love to honor those men who are the *actual*
of the *ideal* in the sacred texts just quoted—the
pedestal of whose honorable and elevated position
has been hewed out of the reluctant granite by
their own labor-loving hands. What is a haughty
duke or earl, with his lofty ancestry running
back through a thousand years, when compared
with an industrious son of labor, whose patent

of nobility is found in his own noble struggles
with early poverty and obscurity? Let the heart
of the young man answer this question!

Permit me to lead you, for a moment, my
reader, into yonder printing-office. Among the
printers are two young men, who are noted for
the unwearied assiduity with which they ply their
daily tasks. Always in the office at the appointed
hour, ever at their posts, toiling with uncom-
plaining steadiness, never yielding to the lassitude
which craves a respite before its work is finished,
they have secured the respect of their employers,
the confidence of their friends, and are slowly
improving their own condition. Concerning these
young men, suppose I predict that they will one
day become widely known and immensely rich.
What do you reply?

You pronounce my prediction an extravagance,
and me a visionary man! Be it so. Yet, under
the guise of this fancy, I have exhibited only a
simple fact. The two young men represent Messrs.
JAMES and JOHN HARPER, who, some thirty years
ago, were poor journeymen printers, but who,

to-day, are owners of one of the most princely publishing establishments in the world. Their names are household words in all civilized communities. And of Mr. James Harper it may be said, that, if not, like the Whittington of our boyish reveries, thrice Lord Mayor of London, he has been once Mayor of the chief city in the great Empire state. But his proudest distinction is, that he and his brother have reared their magnificent house on the foundations of INTEGRITY, ECONOMY, AND INDUSTRY!

The success of industrious effort finds a further illustration in the case of a little boy, named Armstrong, who, a few years ago, entered a Boston printing-office, and labored diligently, as the youngest apprentice, at the lowest tasks of the establishment. Sedulously attending to his duties as they increased in responsibility, he kept on his steady way, till, honorably concluding his apprenticeship, he began business for himself, at the corner of Flag-alley, in State-street. Unwearied in his devotion to his profession, his custom and profits increased. Wealth poured in apace

8

upon him. Honors crowned his brow, and he took his seat, first in the General Court, then in the honorable chair of the Boston mayoralty, and at length in that of the Lieutenant-Governor of Massachusetts. He spent the closing years of his life in a pleasant and stately mansion, an affluent, honorable, and independent man — a noble example of what may be accomplished by the aids of industry.*

The *amount* of profitable labor that a man can healthfully accomplish, during a life of threescore years, can hardly be overrated. The examples of pre-eminently industrious men startle ordinary minds, and they surmise that some friendly hand drew their portraits, and was too lavish in the coloring; but facts are demonstrative that wonders can be accomplished by industry in every department of human life.

WILLIAM COBBETT, whom Ebenezer Elliott designated as England's

"Mightiest peasant born,"

---

* See notice of Lieutenant-Governor Armstrong, by Mr. Buckingham, in the *Boston Courier*.

is an illustration. He was of low birth, and was reared in poverty. While yet a young man, he enlisted in the British army. After serving eight years, he was discharged, and shortly after commenced his political career. From that time to his death, embracing a period of forty-three years — during which he traveled extensively, suffered imprisonments for political offenses, devoted much time to agricultural pursuits, labored incessantly as a political agitator, and finally became a member of the British Parliament — he produced and published no less than *fifty* books of various sizes, and on a variety of topics, besides editing *ninety* volumes of his political papers! the effect of which, on the destinies of England, justifies the strong lines of the lamented Corn-law Rhymer, who thus addresses his memory:

> "Dead oak, thou livest! Thy smitten hands,
>   The thunder of thy brow,
> Speak with strange tongues in many lands,
>   And tyrants hear thee now!"

Now, it is not the character of Cobbett that I commend to your imitation, but his industry.

With all his power, energy, and talent, notwith-standing his pen made the aristocracy of England tremble before its terrible strokes, he was, in my opinion, "a bold, bad man," actuated by passion, hate, and prejudice, rather than by high and holy principles. Still, his laborious diligence is worthy of all commendation, and it is to this, rather than to natural talent, that he himself ascribes his superiority over the millions above whose head he rose to distinction. A diligent husbandry of his time was the talisman by which he achieved his prodigious labors; and this is within the power of every young man, who may also, in his turn, astonish and shame the drones among mankind by the huge measure of his labors, if he will employ his time after the example of William Cobbett.*

Martin Luther, Richard Baxter, John Wesley, Adam Clarke, Richard Watson, Napoleon Bonaparte, Elihu Burritt, and a host beside, might be

---

*For a very fair *critique* on the life and labors of Cobbett, see Stanton's "Sketches of Reforms and Reformers," page 155.

quoted as demonstrations of what may be done by an industrious employment of moments during a lifetime. But what does it avail to multiply examples? Let the young man resolve to become an example himself. Determine to make the most of your opportunities, my young friend; and henceforth act on the principle that moments are grains of gold, by the careful gathering of which you are to become rich in knowledge, in experience, in honor, and in happiness.

It is often objected, that unceasing and assiduous devotion to a round of duties is unfavorable to health. The pale face and emaciated form of the student, the feeble frame of the trembling dyspeptic, and the dying aspect of the flushed consumptive, are pointed out as illustrations of the disastrous influence of toil on the enjoyment and duration of life, and as arguments in favor of self-indulgence and indolent relaxation.

Away with all such pleas and arguments, my young friend! They are the voices of sloth. True, a man may overtax his powers, and injure his health by excessive toil, as was, no doubt, the case with the unfortunate HENRY KIRKE WHITE. He was unwisely ambitious, and attempted tasks with a constitutionally-feeble body, which, with the most robust health, he could scarcely have performed. Such a fact teaches that we must proportion our labors to our capacities — not that we are to sink into supine indulgence, lest we should be sick. Nay, it is not unrelaxing industry, systematically pursued, that pales the face and shortens life. The fact is, that the most industrious men are among the longest livers; and, except where hereditary diseases enfeeble them, are usually healthy. Indeed, industry is favorable to health. There is great meaning in the remark of an eastern missionary, who was laboring incessantly on the translation of the Scriptures into the Hindostan tongue. His friends expostulated with him, and begged him to relax. "Nay," said he; "the man who would live in India must have plenty of work. If not, he will yield to the enervating influence of the climate, and lounge away his days upon the sofa, and consequently be tossing all night on his sleepless couch for want of requisite fatigue. Then comes dejection of spirits and prostration of the whole man."

The missionary was right. Indolence destroys more than industry; and many a drone who has perished prematurely, had his friends been equally honest with Sir Horace Vere, would have had it said of him, as that nobleman said of his brother, when the Marquis of Spinola asked, "Pray, Sir Horace, of what did your brother die?"

"He died of having nothing to do!" was the bluff knight's reply.

When I am told of a sickly student, that he is "studying himself to death," or of a feeble young mechanic or clerk, that his hard work is destroying him, I study his countenance, and there, too, often, read the real, melancholy truth in his dull, averted, sunken eye, discolored skin, pimpled forehead, and timid manner. These signs proclaim that the young man is, in some way, violating the laws of his physical nature. He is *secretly* destroying himself! By sinning against his own body, he is preparing himself for the insane asylum, or for an early grave. Yet, say his unconscious and admiring friends, "He is falling a victim to his own diligence!" Most lame and impotent conclusion! He is sapping the source of life with his own guilty hands, and, erelong, will be a mind in ruins, or a heap of dust. Young man, beware of his example! "Keep thyself pure;" observe the laws of your physical nature, and the most unrelaxing industry will never rob you of a moment's health, nor, in the smallest measure, shorten the thread of your life; for industry and health are companions, and long life is the heritage of diligence.

Behold a cottage at the foot of yonder mountain! On its broken gate sits a lifeless-looking man, with an unstrung bow lying across his knees, and a quiver of arrows strung across his shoulders. A deer, with its delicate young fawn, comes lightly tripping from among the foliage which adorns the mountain slope. Lifting up his heavy eyes, the hunter perceives his prey, and, for a moment, kindles into something like an earnest man. Leaping from the gate, he strains his bow, fixes an arrow on its string, and, gliding from tree to bush, and from bush to tree, approaches the unwatchful deer; then drawing his bow, he lodges an arrow in the heart of the fawn. Seating himself beside it, he triumphs awhile in his success; and then, seeking the shadow of an adjacent tree, slumbers away the day, and permits the burning sun to spoil his venison!

Such is the picture of an idle man, as sketched by Solomon, in these words: "*The slothful man roasteth not that which he took in hunting.*" I have filled up his slender outline, that the young man may study it to better advantage; for, in this instance, at least, the poetic sentiment is literally true, that the monstrous spectacle of vice is sufficient to excite disgust. I greatly misjudge the reader, if he does not heartily despise the idle hunter in the above etching: if he will transfer his scorn to the vice the hunter personates, my end will be accomplished.

To be above the necessity of labor—to spend life in doing nothing—is the fancied paradise of many youthful minds. Yielding to these illusive dreams, they cultivate a hatred for labor; they view the necessity which binds them to the counting-room, or the workshop, as the galley-slave regards his chain. They envy every gay son of pleasure, whose empty laugh is heard ringing through the street: hence, their labor is irksome—their temper sour and repulsive. Their manners become insulting and vexatious to their employers; their incessant complainings annoy their parents, and misery spreads throughout the entire circle of their influence. Thousands of parental hearts are aching at this moment, and thousands of employers are unhappy with their apprentices, solely from this foolish, guilty aspiration after *nothing to do*, which haunts the imaginations of so many young men.

But why do young men pant after an idle life? It is because they are willfully ignorant of the important practical truth, that THE CREATOR COULD HARDLY INFLICT A GREATER CURSE UPON A YOUNG MAN THAN TO DOOM HIM TO A LIFE OF IDLENESS. It would destroy him, soul and body. What is a mind when controlled by idleness? Let the admired Tennyson reply. Personating an idle mind, he says:

> "A spot of dull stagnation, without light
>   Or power of movement, seemed my soul,
> Mid onward sloping motions of the infinite,
>   Making for one sure goal.
>
> A still salt pool, locked in with bars of sand;
>   Left on the shore; that hears all night
> The plunging seas draw backward from the land
>   Their moon-led waters white.
>
> A star that with the choral starry dance
>   Joined not, but stood, and standing saw
> The hollow orb of moving circumstance
>   Rolled round by one fixed law."

If you are ambitious to be "a spot of dull stagnation," "a still salt pool," or a motionless star, be, idle, and you shall assuredly reach the limit of your ambition. But O, it is a costly price to pay for idleness! Nor is the intellect the only sufferer. The heart, the moral character, and even the physical man, share in the dreadful curse. The heart of an idle man is an open common, inviting the presence of every odious vice, which enters in and makes it utterly loathsome. Instead of waiting to be tempted, it "positively tempts the devil;" and while "the busy man is troubled with but one devil, the idle man is visited by a thousand." Idleness first draws its victim from honorable labors, and then whips him into theaters, cafes, gambling-saloons, and darker dens of infamy. It denudes him of all moral beauty and excellency, strips him of self-respect, plunges him into ruin, disease, and degradation; having bound him hand and foot, it plunges his body into an unhonored grave, and consigns his soul to "*everlasting destruction from the presence of the Lord, and from the glory of his power.*" Well hath Holy Writ described the ruin of the indolent man! He began by hating labor, and crying, "*Yet a little sleep, a little slumber, a little folding of the hands to sleep.*" The first visible effect of his sloth was seen in his field and vineyard, "*which was all grown over with thorns, and nettles had covered the face thereof, and the stone-wall thereof was broken down.*" Unalarmed by this growing desolation, the sluggard maintained his hatred of toil, till, as the stroke of war falls upon an unsuspecting hamlet, or a traveler, long on the way, arrives at last, so poverty and want overwhelmed him in irretrievable destruction.

Perhaps my reader replies to this deeply-shaded scene, that such ruin is an extreme case, and not likely to occur to young men generally.   True, it is extreme; but it is equally true that vast numbers of young men annually sink thus from positions of high promise into utter abandonment and destruction.   But admit that the idle youth so trims between sloth and industry as to avoid utter ruin — what then !   He lives a useless, insignificant life.   His place in society is aptly illustrated by certain books in a Boston library, which are lettered "Succedaneum" on their backs. "Succedaneum !" exclaims the visitor; "what sort of a book is that?"   Down it comes; when lo ! a wooden block, shaped just like a book, is in his hands.   Then he understands the meaning of the occult title to be, "In the place of another;" and that wooden book is used to fill vacant places, and to keep genuine volumes from falling into confusion. Such is an idler in society. A man in form, but a block in fact. Living for no high end, giving out no instruction—a dumb, despised "Succedaneum" among mankind.

Nor is this all. Behold such a man drawing nigh to the end of his existence! His pampered and slothful body is tossing upon an uneasy bed. His pale face betokens his approach to the hour of final conflict. His life now passes in sad review before his closing eyes! How like a desert waste it looks! Vainly he searches for some solitary sign that he has not lived in vain. Naught but the dead level of à sandy plain appears. Groaning with anguish, he cries out:

"My life has been as the passage of a ship over the ocean!—as the journey of a pilgrim across a desert! Not a token of my industry, not a trace of my footsteps! No, no more than if my mother had not borne me!"

And with this melancholy utterance, he trembles, shudders, and expires!

And now, young man, having said enough to convince you that your highest interests require of you a life of cheerful labor, I demand your solemn resolve to become a true son of industry. I know all the witcheries of those things which incline you to idleness; the strength of the tendency to sloth in your own breast, and the many failures at self-conquest which are recorded in your past history. But I also know, that if you will seek the aids of *religion*, they will prove sufficient for your utmost needs. Religion will teach you that industry is a SOLEMN DUTY you owe to God, whose command is, Be "DILIGENT IN BUSINESS!" Who says of every disciple of his Son, "*Let him labor, working with his hands the thing which is good, that he may have to give to him that needeth.*" Religion will shed luster upon your meanest toils, by converting them into so many acts of service to almighty God. It will cheer your labors with beams of beauty and glory, from those realms of eternal rest, where employment will be unaccompanied by toil. It will fill your soul with contentment and joy, submission and hope; and arm you with strength to "*come off more than conqueror*" over all foes to industry and purity, *"through Christ who loved you, and gave himself for you."* The burdens of life thus lightened of their weight, you shall endure them cheerfully, so that, whenever you fall in the embrace of death, it may be said of you, in the words of Aldich,

> "His sufferings ended with the day,
>   Yet lived he at its close;
> And breathed the long, long night away
>   In statue-like repose.
>
> But when the sun, in all his state,
>   Illumed the eastern skies,
> He passed through glory's morning gate,
>   And walked in paradise."

CHAPTER VII.

ECONOMY AND TACT.

AS the acquisition of knowledge depends more upon what a man *remembers* than upon the quantity of his reading, so the acquisition of property depends more upon what is *saved* than upon what is *earned*. The largest reservoirs, though fed by abundant and living springs, will fail to supply their owners with water, if secret leaking-places are permitted to drain off their contents. In like manner, though by his skill and energy a man may convert his business into a flowing Pactolus, ever depositing its golden sands in his coffers, yet, through the numerous wastes of unfrugal habits, he may live embarrassed and die poor. Economy is the guardian of property—the good genius whose presence guides the footsteps of every prosperous and successful man.

Economy is a trite and forbidding theme. The

9

young man will feel tempted to pass it by, and proceed to the next chapter. But I beseech him to read on, since his social advancement depends, in a good degree, upon his frugality. He had better be doomed, like the sons of ancient Jacob in Egypt, to make bricks without straw, than to enter the scenes of active life without economy for a companion. Study well, therefore, young man, the following picture :

RALPH MONTCALM is a merchant's clerk, enjoying a fair salary. His age is about twenty-two; his appearance is genteel, without foppishness; his manners are gentlemanly and polite, without affectation. By strict fidelity to the duties of his station, he has gained a high reputation for industry, energy, and integrity. He is also understood to be worth a few hundred dollars, which he has invested with great caution and judgment, where it will yield him a safe and profitable return. The general impression concerning him, among the merchants in his vicinity, is, that he will one day be a man of some importance in society. A shrewd business man remarked, one day, to his employer, " Your clerk has the elements of a successful merchant."

"Yes, sir; Ralph is destined to wield considerable influence 'on change,' one of these days; and being very economical in his habits, he can hardly fail of becoming a rich man."

Such was the reply of Ralph's master. It showed that the clerk was acting on those principles which, in the estimation of experienced men, insure success. Yet Ralph's conduct found no sympathy from the fashionable disciples of dandyism, who filled situations similar to his own, as will be seen by the following conversations.

Ralph was walking home, one evening, from his counting-room, when a fellow-clerk, who was quite an exquisite in his own estimation, overtook him. He was puffing a cigar after the most approved fashion. Stepping up to Ralph, he touched him on the arm, and said,

"Good evening, Mr. Montcalm."

"Good evening, sir," replied Ralph, to this salutation; a few commonplaces passed between them, and then the dandy, taking out his case of Havanas, said,

"Will you take a cigar with me, Mr. Montcalm ?"

"I thank you, sir, but I never smoke!" replied Ralph, with an emphasis which left no room for persuasion.

"Never smoke!" exclaimed the astonished dandy, replacing the cigar-case in his pocket. "What on earth can induce you to deny yourself so delicious a luxury?"

"It is a luxury that costs too much, sir, for me to indulge in it. I really can not afford it."

'O, I see," retorted the smoker, as he puffed forth an enormous column of smoke from his steaming mouth; "you belong to the race of misers, and are set on saving your money, instead of enjoying life as it passes. For my part, I despise all such stinginess, and calculate to enjoy all the pleasure money will buy."

Ralph took no notice of his companion's impolite insinuations, but in a kindly tone answered: "The use of tobacco, in every form, is positively injurious to health and intellect; as a habit, it is filthy, vulgar, and disgusting, to all but those who use it. Beside this, it makes a heavy and constant drain on the purse. I confess, I am too stingy to pay so high a price for a luxury which would shorten my life, fill me with disease, and render me disgusting to others. I would rather save my money for high and noble uses."

This sensible reply was too much for the smoker to endure. He, therefore, gruffly replied: "You talk more like a Puritan than a gentleman;" and hurried forward, leaving Ralph to his reflections, which were certainly more agreeable than the company of such an empty-brained exquisite.

On another occasion, he was thrown into the society of another of these contemptible children of fashion, who, in the course of conversation, inquired,

"Where do you board, Mr. Montcalm?"

"At Mrs. Brown's, in G—— street."

"Indeed! How can you think of boarding in such an unfashionable street?"

"It is my fashion to seek respectability, comfort, cleanliness, and purity, in my home; and all these I have at Mrs. Brown's."

"That may be; but G—— street is such an unfashionable street!—and Mrs. Brown is a poor woman."

"Very true; but still I find genuine comfort, abundant food, and amiable society, at her house; and at a price which I can well afford to pay. What, then, should I gain by going up town to one of your fashionable houses? What do you pay, where you board?"

"I pay rather high in proportion to my salary, to be sure. My board costs me six dollars a week. But then every thing is in style; the boarders are all *fashionable* young men, and I get into some of the highest society in the city through their influence, besides gaining the reputation of being fashionable myself."

"But how do you manage to meet all your expenses? Your salary is only five hundred dollars per annum. You pay over three hundred dollars for board. Your other expenses are in proportion. I do not see how you can ever expect to rise above your clerkship, or even to marry, without saving something for capital; and saving, according to your statements, is out of the question."

"Saving! Don't talk of saving, Mr. Montcalm! I should be very happy to be out of debt. As to business or marriage, I dare not think of either, unless some good-natured merchant should be foolish enough to make me his partner."

"You may well say foolish; for who but a 'good-natured fool' would dream of taking you, or any other slave of fashionable life, into partnership? For myself, I intend both to marry and to enter into business at a proper time. Hence, I can not afford to be a fashionable young man. It costs too much. I prefer the real comfort of a respectable home, and the gains of frugality, to the ruinous reputation of being 'a man of fashion.' I wish you good morning, sir."

'Good morning, Mr. Montcalm," replied the fashionable young gentleman; and they parted, the former to mount the path of honor, the latter to flutter a while, like a stupid moth, around the lamp of fashion, to burn his wings, and then to crawl in obscurity to an unhonored grave.

The reader must view Ralph Montcalm in yet another scene. It is laid in the counting-room of a merchant, with whom Ralph had been transacting some business in his employer's behalf. Just before he left, a gentleman entered on an errand of benevolence. A poor family, in very destitute circumstances, needed aid to keep them from starvation. So stated the visitor, and then he asked,

"Gentlemen, what will you give?"

"Too poor to give!" one of the clerks abruptly replied. He was well known for his love of driving *a la tandem* along the city avenues.

"It costs me so much to live, I can't give any thing!" said another, whose very costly and fashionable attire placed his statement above suspicion.

"Haven't a dollar to spare!" bluntly responded a third, who was remarkable for being almost buried under a load of debts.

"Put me down two dollars," said Ralph, in a half whisper, to the collector, as he quietly handed him that amount.

"How is it that you can afford to give to every one that asks? Your salary is no larger than ours, and yet we can hardly pay our bills. Giving, with us, is out of the question," said the chief clerk to Ralph.

Ralph smiled and replied, "Gentlemen, the difficulty is easily solved. You live high; I live moderately. You are extravagant; I economize. You wear the costliest clothing, and follow every changing fashion; I dress respectably, and avoid extremes. You spend large sums per annum on cigars, wines, riding, theaters, operas, balls, and costly suppers; I deny myself these indulgences, partly because of their cost, and partly because of their immoral tendencies. My pleasures are intellectual; they afford me higher and purer enjoyment than yours, and cost much less. Hence, while you are poor, I have money invested, and something to spare to alleviate the sorrows of others. Good morning, gentlemen."

Such is the example of economy which I desire to urge upon you, young man, for your imitation. Not a miserly meanness, which denies itself the common comforts of life, and shuts itself within walls of triple steel against the appeals of benevolence; but such a manly, generous habit of expending your resources as will tend to improve your condition, without debasing your nature — to make you a man of property, without sinking you to the sordid level of a miser. The principles, which make such admirable economists as young Ralph Montcalm, are:

1. ALWAYS LET YOUR EXPENDITURE BE LESS THAN YOUR INCOME. This is the grand element of success in acquiring property. To carry it out requires resolution, self-denial, self-reliance. But it must be done, or you must be a poor man all through life. If, for example, your income is *six* dollars a week, you must live on *five*, or *four*, if you can with decency. But further:

2. LITTLE EXPENSES MUST BE CAREFULLY GUARDED AGAINST. I once saw a full-grown caterpillar borne along the garden path by an army

of tiny ants, which had made him their captive;
at another time I saw an insect, somewhat resem-
bling a dragon-fly, bearing off a caterpillar by his
own unaided strength. In both cases the victim
perished; and it made little difference whether he
was in the hands of a single dragon-fly, or of an
army of ants. Thus, many little expenses are as
fatal to a young man's prosperity as a great spec-
ulation which ruins at a single blow. The former
will as surely bear him to the grave of poverty as
the latter. Hence, the pence so foolishly spent on
cigars, confectionery, fruit, ice-creams, soda-water,
etc., must be retained in the purse of the young
man who intends to take rank in respectable society. If they escape, they will, in spite of all his
resistance, be like the ant army, and will bear
him to a pauper's grave. *Deny thyself*, in little
as in great things, is a necessary condition of
prosperity.

3. AVOID THE HABIT OF GETTING INTO DEBT.
Attention to the above maxims will make the observance of this one easy. Still, there is, to some
minds, such a fascination in the act of buying on

credit, that they will do it even when they have cash in their pockets. You must avoid this practice. Pay for what you purchase, at least till you begin business; and then buy very cautiously, and you will rarely buy what you do not need. To be in debt is to be enslaved; it is a prolific source of care; an occasion of temptation to extravagance; it often leads to falsehood, dishonesty, gambling, destruction. Debt destroys more than the cholera. Therefore, young man, avoid debt.

4. AVOID LITTLENESS. You saw Ralph Montcalm ready to give to the poor. You must do the same, if not from pure benevolence of feeling, at least out of regard for yourself. Strict economy may lapse into sordid covetousness, and make the frugal man contemptibly mean. I have been told of a wealthy farmer, a professor of religion, who invited a student, just licensed to preach, to stay at his house during a series of religious meetings he was conducting in the neighborhood. When the young preacher was about to leave, the farmer accompanied him to the gate, expressing

great pleasure for his visit and labors. Just before they parted, he said,

"Mr. ——, I should like to make you a small present."

"I thank you, sir," said the young student, bowing acquiescence to the welcome suggestion.

The farmer then took a twenty-five cent coin from his pocket, and said,

"This is the smallest change I have. If you will give me twelve and a half cents in change, you may keep the rest.

'I have no silver about me," replied the student, as he leaped on to his horse, scarcely able to conceal the combined emotions of indignation and merriment which struggled within him for expression.

,If this fact had not been related in my hearing by the aforesaid student, I could hardly have believed that any man could have acted with such contemptible littleness as that farmer; yet such is the meanness of spirit which will grow upon the man whose economy is not joined to some form of benevolent action. Therefore, I repeat the injunction — avoid littleness, by carefully culti-vating a generous, philanthropic spirit, amidst all your plans of frugality.

There is another element of success which is worthy of a few thoughts. I mean *tact*, or versatil-ity — a power of self-adaptation to every new open-ing of Providence. A man of tact immediately fills a new position with naturalness, and, however he himself may feel its embarrassments, he forces the impression upon others that he is just the man for the place. On the other hand, without tact, a man is impracticable. Change his sphere, and he acts stiffly, awkwardly; he is like a stiff-jointed country recruit at his first drill; so uncouth are his movements that lookers-on exclaim, " He will never do !" Hence, his friends lose their interest in his advancement. They fear to advance him, lest his clownishness should mortify their pride. He is left to pine in the obscurity of a lowly po-sition.

But *tact* is the gift of nature. Yes; to some extent it is so. Versatility is easier to some than to others. That is, it requires less effort in some

than in others, to adapt themselves to new relations to society. But even the versatility of the
proudest sons of genius is the offspring of self-
culture. The man who shines in an exalted position, who appears in it with such perfect ease that
one might infer he was born to fill it, has gained
the confidence which inspires him with ease by
previous self-cultivation. A man who is true to
himself is always in advance of his actual position; hence, when called to higher posts, he moves
into them and fills them with propriety and dignity. This is *tact*. And the mental training which
creates tact is within the reach of every young
man.

But what has religion to do with these elements
of success in life? It might as properly be asked,
What has an anchor to do with the safety of a
ship? For, as the latter is held at a secure distance from the shore, notwithstanding the driving
gale, so is a young man bound to the practice of
economy and the cultivation of tact by the authoritative claims of religion. Pride, sensuality, and
custom are like strong winds, beating life's young

voyager upon the rocks of prodigality, or the quicksands of extravagance. Religion anchors him fast, by her strong principles. She exacts diligence, industry, honesty, by her precepts; she pictures the desolation of the spendthrift by her inimitable drawing of the Prodigal Son; she checks waste by teaching the doctrine of accountability to God for all we possess; thundering in every ear her call of *" Give an account of thy stewardship !"* Concerning the duty of fitting one's self to fill his station with honor, the precept of Paul to Timothy is apposite : *" Study to show thyself approved unto God, a workman that needeth not to be ashamed."* And again : *" Give thyself wholly"* to the duties of thy vocation, *"that thy profiting may appear to all."* This exhortation, self-applied by every young man, would constitute him, in a greater or less degree, a man of tact.

Thus does religion in the soul give vigor and fruitfulness to every element of prosperity in human character. Viewed in all its aspects, it justifies the beautiful figure of the good man in the song of the royal psalmist : *" He shall be like a tree planted by the rivers of water, that bringeth forth his fruit in his season: his leaf shall not wither; and whatsoever he doeth shall prosper."*

10

CHAPTER VIII.

HARMONY OF CHARACTER.

THE ABBE MENNAIS has made this beautiful remark: That "from the sun, whence pour inexhaustible floods of light and life, down to the spring that, drop by drop, exudes from the rock, all is ordered for a given end, to which all contribute in an infinite variety of ways, that are the more admired the more they are contemplated. There is not an action, a movement, in the universe, that does not successively contribute to the growth of a tuft of moss."

In this harmony of nature—a harmony so complete and so necessary, that the failure of any one operation in the universe would neutralize the action of all the rest, and denude the earth of its beauty and adornment—we may learn a profitable lesson in relation to the influence of character upon success. In the preceding chapters, I have presented various elements of character in their relation to a prosperous life. They have been treated separately; and, lest the reader should fall into the blunder of supposing that any one of them can *singly* lead to success, I wish to say, with emphasis, that as in the operations of nature, so in the conflicts of life, the effect of great success is produced by the *harmonious combination* of each and every valuable quality. The absence of one qualification may hinder the productiveness of all the rest; the excess of another may undo all that the proper action of the rest had accomplished. For example, let a young man be industrious, versatile, energetic, intelligent, and yet lack integrity, what becomes of his prosperity? He *may* acquire wealth by dishonest means, but he must live without the confidence of good men, and die *"as the fool dieth."* Or, suppose him to have integrity, intelligence, industry, economy, and to be defective in energy, he will sink, in spite of all his high qualifications, beneath the obstacles which lie in every man's path to eminence. Or, again, let him have an excess of energy, he will be rash and fall into irretrievable ruin; let him be excessively frugal, and he will become a miser; let him be over versatile, he will be the "rolling stone which gathers no moss;" an excessive attachment to letters will convert him into a theorist or a book-worm. Thus, it is apparent, that, to insure success, a young man must diligently attain, and prudently cultivate, all those particular excellences which, when possessed in combination, make a failure next to impossible.

What reader of holy Scripture has not felt a most tender regard for that interesting youth, who, in all the eagerness of self-confidence, stood complacently before the great Teacher and asked,

"*Good Master, what shall I do to inherit eternal life?*"

With what elation of soul did that young self-deceiver listen to the reply of the great Heart-searcher: "*If thou wilt enter into life, keep the commandments!*"

Exulting in his fancied triumph, the young man replied, "*All these I have kept from my youth up ! What lack I yet ?*"

By one stroke — a stroke severely kind — the Redeemer prostrated all his hopes: "YET LACKEST THOU ONE THING !" And then he gave him a practical test, which at once unfolded his true state to his startled mind, and convinced him that, however externally spotless he might be, his heart was supremely selfish. He lacked that self-devotion to the glory of God which is the essence of all true religion — a lack that neutralized all his excellences, and was fatal to his confidence in the Divine favor.

Young man, you may, in like manner, fail of true greatness through one fatal deficiency, and be ranked with the men so fitly described by the great English bard:

> "Men
> Carrying, I say, the stamp of one defect,
> Their virtues else—be they as pure as grace,
> As infinite as man may undergo—
> Shall, in the general censure, take corruption
> From that particular fault."

LORD BYRON'S history furnishes a most painful example of the ruin resulting from the want of symmetry in character. To use the splendid diction of MACAULAY, "He was born to all men covet and admire. But in every one of those eminent advantages which he possessed over others, there was mingled something of misery and debasement. He was sprung from a house, ancient, indeed, and noble, but degraded and impoverished by a series of crimes and follies. The young peer had great intellectual powers; yet there was an unsound part in his mind. He had naturally a generous and tender heart, but his temper was wayward and irritable. He had a head which statuaries loved to copy, and a foot the deformity of which the beggars in the street mimicked. He was distinguished by the strength and by the weakness of his intellect; affectionate, yet perverse—a poor lord, and a handsome cripple."

What was the result of these opposite combinations?—of this lack of moral symmetry? The first noticeable efforts of his muse, being directed by his perverse temper, brought him a harvest of contempt and hatred. Stung to the quick, he exerted his noble genius, and produced a composition which raised him to the pinnacle of fame; and "all this world, and all the glory of it, were at once offered to him." Like a spoiled child, he now yielded to the violence of his passions, and the bitterness of his temper. For this society cast him out of its pale. He fled to Italy, and there, by turns, cultivated his genius and gratified his passions. He lost his health, his hair became gray, his food ceased to nourish him. The Grecian struggle for independence roused, for a time, his nobler sentiments. He dragged his diseased body to Missolonghi; and there, at the age of thirty-six, this "most celebrated Englishman of the nineteenth century, closed his brilliant and miserable career."

Who will deny that Lord Byron's life was a splendid failure? Why was it so? Not for lack of high qualities of mind, but through excess of low and degraded passions. Had this unhappy man subdued his evil qualities, and sedulously cultivated what was high and noble in his nature, his name would have passed down to posterity as a model of all excellency and beauty. Neglecting this, he stands among the images of the past, like some grim ghost on the great highway of life, scaring the advancing traveler from the ways of self-neglect and self-indulgence.

To resist temptations, to be prepared for all emergencies, to rise to real eminence, to answer life's great end, you must avoid the example before you. You must cultivate all the conditions of success, and especially those in which you find yourself most deficient. See to it, that there are neither excesses nor defects in your character, but a harmonious blending, a delightful symmetry, formed of fitting proportions of every high quality.

How shall this symmetry of character be attained? By what means shall the young man repress his low and debasing qualities, develop what is noble and beautiful in human nature, and maintain a due proportion of each element of social superiority? This is a great question. I will attempt its solution.

Figure to your mind a perfect circle; observe that its perfection depends upon the equidistance of every part of its line from the point in its center. The least deviation would destroy its perfectibility. Harmony of character is, in like manner, produced by the action of some great central principle upon the conduct — a principle whose comprehensive grasp reaches to every act and feeling, regulating, stimulating, repressing, or guiding, as circumstances may require. Such a principle, standing like the central point in the circle, and wielding absolute authority over the soul, is the only sure means of producing that harmony of character so essential to success.

The stern heroism of REGULUS, the Roman general, may serve to illustrate the influence of such a principle. This brave soldier, after being defeated, and kept in captivity for several years, was sent by the Carthaginians with an embassy to Rome, to solicit a cessation of arms and an exchange of prisoners. To secure his influence in their favor, they made him swear that, if the desired end was not attained, he would return to Carthage. The Roman took the oath, and departed.

Touched with the misfortunes of their general, the Roman senate was disposed to treat for peace, and retain the heroic Regulus. But he, knowing the weakness and exhaustion of Carthage, boldly advised the continuance of the war. Upon this, the senate rejected the overtures of the embassadors; and, knowing the fate which awaited their general, entreated him to remain at Rome. His wife, his children, his friends, with tears and embraces, besought him not to rush on certain destruction. He was inexorable. He had sworn to return, and no considerations could change his iron purpose to keep his oath. He did return, and his ungenerous foes, to their eternal infamy, put him to death in the most cruel and malignant manner.

What was it that made Regulus proof against the tears of his friends, the love of his wife, the affection of his children, the fear of death? — for he resisted all these to fulfill his oath. Was he an unfeeling stoic? Nay! but he was animated by that noble principle of Roman honor, which taught that death was preferable to a false, a mean, or a dastardly action! And it was this controlling sentiment, expelling or subduing all others, which led him to prefer his heroic death to the violation of a Roman's word. It also preserved him from sacrificing the interests of his country to his own safety. It made him at once a patriot and a hero.

Thus, you may perceive that the influence of a noble principle is like the action of the centripetal force on the solar system. As that attractive energy steadily maintains the unity and order of the universe, so a lofty, comprehensive, authoritative principle subdues the thoughts, emotions, and actions to itself, and maintains a delightful harmony in the life of a young man, which commands the admiration and confidence of mankind. It is the wave-line of beauty, which, running through all his conduct, imparts gracefulness to each act, and dignity and propriety to his entire character.

It is, therefore, a question of great moment to

every young man, where to obtain a principle
sufficiently comprehensive and powerful to regulate all the parts of his conduct, so as to form one
harmonious whole. Some are satisfied with the
sentiment of *honor*, such as ruled the Roman patriot. But that is obviously not sufficiently comprehensive. Your modern *men of honor* are gam-
blers, duelists, tyrants, Sabbath-breakers, drunk-
ards, speculators, and the like ; such things not
being prohibited in the code of honor as established by public opinion, and the conduct of
"great men," falsely so called. Neither is the
law of *self-respect* sufficient. It doubtless does
much to regulate life in the sphere of home, but
is not proof against the temptations which assail
men when abroad. Look, for instance, to the
alarming fact, that the theaters, brothels, and
other places of sinful resort in large cities, are
chiefly supported by persons from the country.
And who are these men from interior towns ?
What are they, when at home, but rigid moralists
in appearance ? Diligent, self-denying men in
their general habits, but immoral on occasions

and opportunities. The reason is obvious. They are restrained among their friends only by that low standard of self-respect which fears degradation in the eyes of others, but shrinks not from being mean in its own eyes, and guilty in the sight of God. It is not at all surprising, that such a flimsy defense against temptation often yields to a fierce and persevering assault.

A fearful illustration of the absolute powerlessness of these restraints, when the soul is powerfully tempted, is furnished in the case of the late Professor Webster. If ever mortal man was placed in a situation to maintain a high character, through motives of self-respect and honor, he was that man. Educated, highly respectable in his connections, moving in the most refined and elevated circles in social life, widely known through his connection with the mother of American universities, the husband of an accomplished wife, the father of amiable, lovely daughters, and the possessor of what ought to have been an ample income — how could he fail of feeling, in their full force, the claims of honor and the demands of self-respect? For him to do a notoriously-mean or unlawful act, was to fall from the loftiest pinnacle of social honor to the lowest valley of shame. He knew this: hence, honor and self-respect combined to keep him within the bounds of right and truth. But, alas! how ineffectual were these restraints! Failing to reach the inner temple of the soul, they left him a prey to pride, extravagance, and passion. Pushed by pride into extravagance, and by extravagance into embarrassments, and by these again into acts of meanness, which, if proclaimed, would wound his haughty pride, his passions urged him to strike the desperate blow of murder, to free himself from the threatening danger. Passion won the day. He slew Patroclus, but fell into the hands of Achilles. By striking a man from existence, whom he deemed his tormentor, he became a felon, and was dragged by the stern hand of the law from his high position to the scaffold! Alas! that his self-respect and his sense of honor should have failed to keep him from moral deformity and from crime! That it did not is an obvious fact; and that it *can not* be relied upon in the hour when the tempter does his utmost, is equally demonstrable, from the nature of the case, and from the history of mankind.

Far higher, therefore, must that young man look than mere honor or self-respect, who would attain to symmetry and stability of character. RELIGION alone can furnish him with a principle at once potent and comprehensive enough for his stern necessities. Religion establishes itself on the throne of the soul. It exerts its restraining and transforming power over the will, the intellect, and the emotions. It persuades, entreats, and it also commands with Divine authority. It lays the soul under the weightiest obligation to walk by its great, all-embracing principle. "WHETHER, THEREFORE, YE EAT OR DRINK, OR WHATSOEVER YE DO, DO ALL TO THE GLORY OF GOD."

Here is a far-reaching principle, laying every act, thought, and motive under contribution; demanding the utter negation of self, and the subordination of the entire man, physical and spiritual.

to the law of God. As the mysterious magnet points unerringly to the northern pole of the earth, so does this law direct the soul of the young man to "*the glory of God.*" He must repudiate whatever act or thought dishonors his Creator; he must resolutely practice every thing, however it may crucify the passions, which tends to glorify the God of heaven. Here, then, is a principle suited to his necessities, whose operation, if submitted to, must, from the nature of the case, produce a lovely symmetry of character. It will bind and restrain unlawful passion, create integrity—stimulate to energy, to self-culture, to industry, to economy, to tact, to every thing that develops noble qualities and latent powers. Nor are its requisitions of impossible performance. The same authority which announces the law also vouchsafes power to obey. "Ye shall receive power from on high!" "My grace is sufficient for thee," are the encouraging promises of the Lawgiver to every willing recipient of his command. And so effectually is that aid vouchsafed to every submissive and believing mind, that, filled with conscious power, it can view all the temptations of the inner and outer life, and exclaim, "I can do all things through Christ, who strengtheneth me!"

To religion, therefore, young man, do I earnestly commend you, as the surest means of attaining harmony of character. Only let the "glory of God run like a silver thread through all your actions," and you shall stand forth before the world a symmetrical man, and, hence, a man of power; for

"'Tis moral grandeur makes the mighty man."

11

CHAPTER IX.

VICE AND ITS ALLUREMENTS.

DANTE, in his DIVINA COMEDIA, describes a broad-shouldered mountain rising before him, directly after he had gone astray "from the path direct." Resolute of purpose, he prepared to journey "over that lonely steep;" but he says:

> "Scarce the ascent
> Begun, when lo! a panther, nimble light,
> And covered with a speckled skin, appeared;
> Nor when it saw me vanished; rather strove
> To check my onward going."

Having overcome this beast, he adds:

> "A lion came 'gainst me as it appeared,
> With his head held aloft and hunger mad,
> That e'en the air was fear-struck. A she-wolf
> Was at his heels, who in her lameness seemed
> Full of all wants."

Trembling before this new enemy, he was about

to flee, when a form appeared, who, in reply to his tears and entreaties, said :

"Thou must needs
Another way pursue, if thou wouldst 'scape
From out that savage wilderness. This beast
To whom thou criest, her way will suffer none
To pass; and no less hind'rance makes than death."

The panther of Dante, with its soft, gay skin, is an emblem of voluptuousness in all its forms. The lion is the figure of ambition; the wolf, of avarice. These three beasts beset and assail every traveler in the way of life. First comes the panther, when the passions wake to life in the young man's breast, striving to destroy him with the pleasures of lust and appetite. If by these means he is conquered — if he permits himself to be charmed by illicit, sensual gratifications — he sinks to the level of a brute; and his body, his name, and deeds speedily rot together. If he resist the panther, the insatiable cravings of ambition wake up, fierce as a lion, in his soul, and he is tempted to enter the lists where men do tilt, and tourney for the crowns of human fame. For these, if am-

bition triumph, he forfeits the crown of everlasting life. Should he resist, and seek distinction only as a means of honoring his Creator, the
wolf of avarice next seeks his overthrow. Thus
danger succeeds danger, till he perishes, or, by
resistance and conquest, attains a noble sublimity
of character; and, radiant in the rays of a virtue
gained through the power of a religious faith,
passes in triumph through the "everlasting doors"
into the eternal paradise.

You, young man, are at the age in which the
passions and appetites begin to clamor for indulgence. They glow with all the fervor of fierce
desire, and prompt you to indulge yourself through
means forbidden both by the constitution of your
nature and the laws of God. Remember that
your Creator has implanted these propensities
within you for high and holy purposes. They
are not necessarily debasing and imbruting in
their tendencies. They only become so when,
impatient of restraint, a youth lays the reins of
control upon their neck, and bids them dash, with
wild impetuosity, across the Rubicon which flows

along the borders between innocence and guilt,
right and wrong. But when, by the aids of
reason and conscience, the triumphant soul becomes conscious of holding a high moral reign
over the inferior body, it rapidly rises in dignity
and in power. The very strength of these propensions, by calling the authority of the soul
into existence, thus serves to promote its elevation and develop its greatness. Determine, therefore, young reader, to be above the servitude of
the senses. Let your intelligent soul, aided by
Divine grace, point to the limit of Divine law,
and say to the foamings of passion, as God to
the swelling sea, "*Hitherto shalt thou come, but
no further; and here shall thy proud waves be
stayed!*" and the grace of Christ shall shut up
your desires, as his omnipotence has "*shut up the
sea with doors.*"

One of your chief dangers, in this controversy
with passion, is found in the fact that while religion, conscience, duty, cry, "RESTRAIN! DENY!"
the world, through its pleasures and its adherents,
cries, "ENJOY!" Hence, temptations and prac-

tical sanctions to vicious indulgence abound. Corresponding to the burning desires within, are abundant means to gratify them without. These means are so contrived as to hide the *miseries* of vice beneath dazzling and charming appearances. That wretched poet, BYRON, who wrote from the black depth of his own tormented spirit, thus describes it in his "CHILDE HAROLD:"

> "Ah vice! how soft are thy voluptuous ways!
> While boyish blood is mantling, who can 'scape
> The fascination of thy magic gaze!
> A cherub hydra round us dost thou gape,
> And mold to every taste thy dear, delusive shape."

Behold by yonder wayside a small and delicate tree, covered with a rich profusion of crimson bloom. As you stand at a distance, it strongly resembles a peach-tree covered with its beautiful blossoms. A nearer approach will undeceive you. Heaps of dead insects at your feet, and swarms of living ones floating round its bloom, and hastening to sip its fatal nectar, proclaim the poisonous nature of the gaudy shrub. Yon passing peasant boy will tell you it is the "Judas-tree," or, in Indian phraseology, the "Red-bud."

Such is vice to every young novitiate — charming to the eyes, exquisitely exciting to the senses, it allures the unwary youth to taste its forbidden pleasures. He sees the brilliant gayety of the saloon and the theater. He hears the soft, voluptuous music of the orchestra and the ball-room. He gazes on the radiant faces of the dancers, and on the excited crowds who throng the portals of the drama. He observes the seductive glances of the "strange woman," till his blood boils, his head reels, his desires overcome him. "There *is* pleasure in these things," he cries. Then, heedless of the admonishing shade of his mother, which gazes sadly on his tempted spirit, scorning the monition of his moral guardian — his conscience, which cries "Forbear" — reckless of all but present joy, he flies to taste the forbidden nectar. One taste only inflames his soul the more. Like the insects on the Judas-tree, he heeds not the swarms of perished ones, but tastes and tastes again, till he is lost beyond redemption.

Stand with me, in imagination, young man, at the hour of midnight, and gaze upon the fire in yonder city. A large cluster of houses is wrapped in flames, which, roaring aloud, as if rejoicing in destruction, send their broad, red sheets and their ever-darting fiery tongues far up into the gloomy sky. At length they spread to an aviary containing nearly a thousand beautiful canary-birds. Unable to remove them, unwilling to stand and see them burned, their owner opens the doors of their prison-house, and the bewildered birds fly into the air. Mounted above the flames, they hover for a while in seeming safety. Now they whirl in circles above the fearful blaze, as if held by some irresistible fascination; now, sweeping downward and upward, as if irresolute of purpose, they linger a little longer, till first one and then another drops into the burning pile, and every little songster is speedily destroyed.

Very similar are the fascinations of vicious pleasures. Once within the embrace of evil, a young man has little hope of escape. If he will not study its terrible consequences, before he enters upon its practice, he will be either blind to their existence, or so fascinated by the spell exerted over his passions, that his escape will be next to an impossibility. So deadly is the infatuation of vice to a fallen young man, that the first indulgence by which he enters the path of the sensualist might almost claim the lines which DANTE has inscribed over the gate of hell:

> " Through me you pass into the city of woe,
> Through me you pass into eternal pain,
> Through me, among the people lost for aye.
>
>   o   o   o   o
>
> All hope abandon ye who enter here."

This is speaking very strongly, I am aware; because the sensualist, whether drunkard, debauchee, or glutton, *may* be pardoned and regenerated through the atonement of Jesus Christ He *may*, such is the all-abounding grace of Christ, escape the bondage of vice, and win the freedom of a man of virtue. But the enervating influence and the ever-increasing potency of

vicious indulgences are so great and so mighty,
that there is little room to hope for the recovery
of a young man, who, having been trained to pure
principles, descends to the corruptions of a bad
life. Vice is like the terrible cobra di capello,
which winds itself round its victim, and from its
deadly fangs pours poison into his blood. So
vice enslaves and destroys. Whoever is charmed
to its embraces, finds himself infolded in bonds
of might, and poisoned with a morbid venom
which irritates and stimulates his passions beyond
the endurance of his vital powers; till, with a
diseased body, a hardened heart, and a remorseful spirit, he sinks to an untimely death, and is
driven to stand, shivering with fear, before his
God.

The history of mankind is a great commentary
upon this truth. It is crowded with cases of
those who, through the allurements of the passions, have madly rushed on ruin. They have
seen fortune, fame, station, reputation, and even
empire, sliding away beneath their feet. Voices
of friendship have stunned their ears with warn-

ings. Ruin, with grim and horrid visage, has
stared them in the face. But, spell-bound, enchanted, charmed, they have heedlessly pursued
their pleasures,

> "Like birds the charming serpent draws,
> To drop head foremost in his jaws,"

till the darkness of the second death swallowed
them up forever!

Do you ask for particular examples? Let me
lead you to that of MARK ANTONY, one of the
triumviri who governed Rome after the assassin-
ation of Cæsar. He was the possessor of high
military talents, the idol of his soldiers, the husband of the nobly-born Octavia, and one of the
chiefs of the greatest empire in the world. This
man, as you know, was met, in the fullness of his
strength and in the pride of his victories, by the
luxurious Cleopatra, Queen of Egypt. Lured by
her voluptuous wiles, he yielded himself up to
a life of sensuous prodigality. The feast, the
dance, the song, absorbed his time; the artifice
and beauty of Cleopatra captivated his soul.

Regardless of honor and duty, he divorced his wife; reckless of consequences, he wasted his resources, neglected his fortunes, and saw without concern the preparations of his rival, Octavius, to secure his ruin. He lay, a self-abandoned victim, in the arms of his artful destroyer. No sense of honor, no idea of self-respect, no fear of overhanging consequences, could rouse him from his fatal entrancement. But the cloud soon burst over his foolish head, and in the midst of the storm, he lost empire, fame, and life together.

Poor ROBERT BURNS, the bard of Scotland, is another illustration of the *power* of vice to retain its victim. His talents raised him from the obscurity of his early life to distinction. His generous independence of mind secured him the affections of those with whom he became intimate. With ordinary prudence, he might have spent his days in ease and independence. But his noble spirit was in the bonds of dissipation. Many, but vain, were his struggles after freedom. Innumerable were his resolves to conquer the habit which charmed and disgusted him by turns. The consciousness he felt concerning the utter hopelessness of his case, is touchingly expressed in the following lines, composed by himself, as a prayer, in a fit of dangerous illness:

> " Fain would I say, 'Forgive my foul offense,'
>   Fain promise never more to disobey ;
> But should my Author health again dispense,
>   Again I might desert fair virtue's way,
>   Again in folly's path might go astray,
> Again exalt the brute and sink the man;
>   Then how should I for heavenly mercy pray,
> Who act so counter heavenly mercy's plan —
> Who sin so oft have mourned, yet to temptation ran !"

This melancholy subjection of soul to sense continued to the close of his life. His last illness was brought on by the dissipation of a winter's night. He died in poverty, the victim of a folly which weakened his powers, dimmed the luster of his fame, and shortened his days on earth. Pitiful sight, to see a soul possessed of such noble powers enslaved by a degrading vice! How forcibly does the ruin of such minds prove the almost omnipotence of vice!

The case of RICHARD BRINSLEY SHERIDAN, the most brilliant orator of his times, is equally in point. What native greatness must have held its seat in his soul! What magnificence of intellect was that which gave birth to the eloquence, wit, and argument, which drew from the glorious Burke the confession that the effect of his speech, in the case of Warren Hastings, was the "most astonishing of any of which there was any record or tradition;" and from the great Mr. Pitt, the acknowledgment that it "surpassed all the eloquence of ancient or modern times." Yet even his great soul was the slave of imperious passions. Indolence, dissipation, prodigality, held him bound in chains of steel, and bore him to distress, anguish, poverty, and ruin. Vain were all his agonizing struggles after his lost moral freedom. This man, whose eloquence led princes to court his friendship, and compelled the admiration of his rivals in politics and oratory, was arrested by a sheriff's officer for debt, on his death-bed. What invincible strength! What irresistible attractions! What power to debase and to weaken must be lodged in vices which could pull down ruin on the head of such a princely intellect as that of Richard Brinsley Sheridan!

I have given these illustrations from the lives of what are called great men, that the young man may see the power of vice over minds of the largest capacity. If such men found it impossible to escape, how can others encourage the hope of a better fate? Nay, dear youth, the only safe course for you is to RESOLUTELY LET ALL VICIOUS INDULGENCE ALONE. "*Avoid it, pass not by it, turn from it, and pass away: then shalt thou walk in thy way safely, and thy foot shall not stumble.*"

The plea of every young mind that enters upon its novitiate in the school of vice, is for only a little self-indulgence. The mind, while undefiled by positive contact with the sins of the senses, revolts from the idea of a wholly-vicious life. It views such a life as the dogs of Egypt are said to fear the crocodiles which abound in the Nile. So intense is this fear, that, when impelled by fierce thirst to drink its waters, they do it as they run, not daring to pause long enough at once to satisfy their burning desires. Thus does the young man propose to taste illicit joys. He would only *taste* and flee, lest he should be devoured. Alas! he knows not the terrible power he awakens, when he quaffs his first draught from the prohibited stream of pleasure! By that one act, he casts away the talisman of his safety, self-denial; he removes the curb from the mouth of lust, he pours foul water upon the virgin snow, and thus places an ineffable stain upon his purity; he contracts guilt, sows the seed of remorse, and sells his moral freedom for naught. A little indulgence? Never, young man! Allow it, and you are lost; blindness begins where vice first enchants. Beware, O beware of this pestilential apology! Be like the knights of Tasso, who, on Armida's enchanted isle, seeing all the enticements of sense voluptuously prepared and inviting to indulgence, exclaimed:

"Let us avoid the dream
Of warm desire, and in resolve be strong;

Now shut our ears to the fair siren's song,
And to each smile of feminine deceit
Close the fond eye."

Thus resolved, the wiles and witcheries of Armida's luxurious groves and bewitching damsels were powerless; for

" To these wiles the knights in triple steel
Of stern resolve had shut their souls ; and, hence,
The tunes they sing, the beauties they reveal,
Their angel looks and heavenly eloquence,
But circle round and round, nor reach the seat of sense."

Thus must every young man meet the *first* advances of vicious solicitation, if he would not be drawn into hopeless servitude. The saying of an odd writer, concerning courts of law, is applicable to the court of pleasure. He says, "A man who goes to law finds the court full of invisible hooks. He turns round to disembarrass himself from one, and straightway he is caught by another. First his cloak, then the skirts of his coat, then his sleeves, till erelong every thing is torn from him,

12

and, like a gipsy, he escapes because he is so stripped there is no further hold upon him."

The youth who crosses the threshold of the court of vice will find these "invisible hooks" sharper and in greater abundance than in courts of law. Once caught, he will be *"hooked"* in every direction. One tempter will succeed another, each handing him over to the next. Thus snared and dragged from vice to vice, till denuded of every virtue, he will at last, in all probability, perish in unutterable woe. Therefore, young reader, beware of the *first* lesson in vice! Your escape from destruction depends on your being strong in resolve to resist the first advances of illicit pleasure. "The bird which is insnared by one leg is as surely the prey of the fowler as if it were seized by both wings." Or let one wheel of a watch be magnetized, it will attract all the other wheels to itself, and thus as effectually destroy its correctness as if every wheel was displaced. Beware, then, of one disordered passion— one insnaring abomination!

I find a very appropriate illustration of the risk

incurred by one indulgence in forbidden things in the life of the great Arabian impostor, MOHAMMED. In the course of his astonishing career of victory, he captured the citadel of Khaibar. A Jewish captive, named Zainab, determined to destroy the conqueror. To accomplish her purpose, she prepared a subtile poison, an art in which she was exquisitely skillful, and introduced it into a shoulder of lamb, which was designed for the prophet's table. Her plot was undiscovered, and in due time the poisoned meat was set before the intended victim. Unsuspicious of danger, Mohammed began his repast. But at the first mouthful, perceiving something unusual in its taste, he spit it forth; but instantly felt acute internal pain. In that brief moment he had imbibed enough of the poison to injure his constitution through the remainder of his life. Many were the severe paroxysms of pain he suffered from its potency. And in his dying moments, while undergoing intense physical agony, he exclaimed:

"The veins of my heart are throbbing with the poison of Khaibar!"

Young man! believe me, your first taste of vicious pleasure, though it may not be succeeded by a second offense, may be as fatal to you as the poison of Zainab was to the oriental prophet. HORACE MANN, in his noble "Thoughts for a Young Man," has well said: "The capital of health may be all forfeited by one physical misdemeanor." He might have added, that the capital of character, of moral purity, of self-respect, are all jeopardized by one transgression. Pause, therefore, at the threshold of the temple of infamy; and though a jovial companion, a witching seducer, may say, "*Only this once!*" do you reflect and reply: "Nay! on a death-bed the veins of my heart may throb with the poison of this one sin."

"*Wherewithal shall a young man cleanse his way?*" was the question of the Psalmist, when viewing, as we have been doing, the allurements and power of vice. The question is timely and proper at this stage of our work. The answer of the experienced minstrel is equally in point; namely, "*By taking heed thereto* ACCORDING TO

THY WORD;" that is, by securing the aid of religious power. Without this help from above, such
is the tyranny of human passion and appetite,
resistance is almost vain. Wrestling with their
strength, the unaided youth will be compelled to
exclaim, with a greater than himself, " *O, wretched
man that I am! who shall deliver me from the
body of this death!*" If, like that majestic apostle, he will fly to the grace of Christ, he will be
enabled to join in his triumphal strains, and cry,
" *Nay, in all these things we are more than conquerors through him that loved us!*" and again : " *This
one thing I do—I keep my body under, and bring
it into subjection.*"

Fly, therefore, beloved young man, to the ark
of our divine religion for safety. There the energy, the strength, the power of an inner life
shall be developed within you. Satisfied from
within yourself, fortified by strong affection for
virtue, and intense loathing against vice, you will
be secure. Your character shall thus be lofty;
your purity unspotted; your real enjoyment un-
diminished, yea, immeasurably increased; your

name, instead of being "writ in water," shall be
engraved on the hearts of the good, and in the
records of eternity.

CHAPTER X.

VICE AND ITS CONSEQUENCES.

WITH what graphic beauty has the pencil of MOSES sketched the scenes of patriarchal life! How true to human nature, how instructive to a thoughtful mind, are his delineations of those ancient characters! But their highest encomium is their unquestionable truthfulness. Let us study one of these pictures, and carefully extract its precious moral.

Behold the venerable ABRAHAM standing in the doorway of his tent, with his vigorous and manly nephew, LOT, at his side! Lot is deeply agitated. The uneasy workings of restrained anger are visible in his flashing eye, knitted brows, and earnest manner. Let us listen to his words:

"Revered sire, our herdmen are at war with each other. Every day their contentions increase!

Their strifes are not to be endured! What can be done?"

Abraham, calm and dignified, replies, "Let there be no strife, I pray thee, between me and thee, for we be brethren. Is not the whole land before thee? Separate thyself, I pray thee, from me. If thou wilt take the left hand, I will go to the right; or, if you depart to the right hand, I will go to the left!"

Upon this, Lot gazes at the lovely landscape spread out around them. It embraces the fertile vale of the Jordan, rich in its herbage, its wells, and fruits. True, the vile inhabitants of Sodom live on its borders. But Lot has a worldly heart. He seeks only to be rich: hence, on selfish and sinful principles alone, he selects the valley of the Jordan, and, separating himself from his uncle, takes up his abode in the vale of Sodom, intent on acquiring and enjoying riches. Abraham removed his tent to Hebron.

Scarcely has Lot established himself in his new home, before an invading army sweeps over the vale, and Lot, with his family and flock, is led away a prisoner. Abraham, with his good sword, hastens to his rescue, and he is restored. For a while, Lot now enjoys prosperity; but his children mostly fall into the vices of the place, and apostatize from God. The hour of Sodom's overthrow then arrived. Through the intercession of Abraham, Lot is warned of the impending danger, and, leaving all his wealth and most of his children behind, he flees penniless to the mountains. On the way, his wife falls by the hand of God; and poor, destitute Lot, with two of his daughters, becomes the forlorn occupant of a mountain cave! How different was this result from the sanguine expectation which swelled his breast on the day when, for mere purposes of profit and enjoyment, he pitched his tent beside the gate of Sodom!

What a melancholy lesson lies on the surface of this sketch! How emphatically it teaches the doom of a worldly mind to disappointment! How like a warning voice should the fate of Lot ring in the ears of the youth who is looking out upon the vale of life, and regarding the enchanting

devices of evil with a strength of desire brooking
no restraint! The song, the dance, the revel, the
theater, the saloon, the gaudy sepulcher of departed virtue, all blend in the gay pictures of his
fancy; and he, like Lot, deliberately resolves to
take up his abode in the vale of modern Sodom.
Not that he intends to be as vile as others. O,
no! He is a perfect HAZAEL, contemplating vicious excess with a stern indignation which cries,
"Is thy servant a dog, that he should do this thing?"

It is from limited indulgence he anticipates a
harvest of delight. But, limited or excessive, the
result is the same. Sinful pleasure, in all its Pro-
tean shapes, disappoints its victim. From the first
delirious, intoxicating draught, to the last dreg in
the cup, all is *disappointment.* Hear a veteran in
the ranks of folly testify:

> " When all is won that all desire to woo,
> The paltry prize is hardly worth the cost.
> Youth wasted, mind degraded, honor lost,
> These are thy fruits, successful passion—these!
> If, kindly cruel, early hope is crost,
> Still to the last it rankles, a disease
> Not to be cured when love itself forgets to please."

· But why, if the first experiences of young profligates are succeeded by disappointment, do they
persist? Because they vainly hope that other
untried indulgences will yield greater pleasure.
They fear the contempt of their more daring
associates, but chiefly because passion is a tyrant,
a perfect Haynau. When once freed from the
golden chain of innocence, it usurps absolute authority, and drives its victim, like a helpless slave,
to ruin. The drunkard knows but too well the
terrible power of his ever-craving appetite. His
reason, his affections, his self-respect, his dearest
friends, his present and eternal interests, all stand
at the bar of this inward monster, and plead in
vain. It impels him, in spite of himself, to sink
into deeper misery. The same is true of every
other vicious habit. He who enters upon a vicious
career, is like the man who is lured by a false
light to venture on the treacherous quagmire;
once sunk in its fatal mud, every attempt to extricate himself only sinks him still deeper. Terrible,
indeed, are his efforts, awful his apprehensions,
fearful is his prospect of destruction. If he does

escape, it is as if by miracle. "He is *carnal, sold under sin.*" He has surrendered the helm of his soul to his baser nature. Nothing short of a complete abandonment of himself to religion can restore that lost helm to the hand of reason. That step he will not take, and, therefore, he *can not* pause in his wicked career. And this is one portion of a sinner's penalty. The pleasure he invited as a guest to beguile his hours of leisure, becomes his master. He sees his ruin, yet rushes upon it. Abject, stung to the quick, irritated, agonized, and tortured, he writhes in vain struggles to free himself from his tyrant. Despondency seizes his mind, and often, as in the melancholy case of the late Dr. Morton, a young English physician, he concludes the tragedy by rushing, an unbidden guest, into the spirit-world.

This Dr. Morton, who appears to have been a man of genius, had fallen into the vice of drunkenness. Many and fierce were his vain struggles for the mastery, as may be seen by the following extract from his journal:

"I have only to remember my dreadful sufferings the morning after taking so much beer or wine. Low suicidal feelings, despondent and gloomy thoughts, pulse one hundred to one hundred and twenty, head dizzy, limbs tremulous, pains about the heart, flatulence and eructations, incapacity for duty of any kind, temper irritable and overbearing, expensive habits, loss of time, forgetfulness of engagements, every thing in disorder — and all for what ? *Because I choose to take two pints of ale, or half a bottle of wine.*"

As already intimated, this accomplished but unhappy man, finding himself enslaved to his darling vice, died by his own hand at the early age of thirty-six — a sad monument of the terrible effect of vice on a superior mind !

BYRON has well described this despairing gloom which, sooner or later, overspreads the sinning soul :

> "And vice, that digs her own voluptuous tomb,
> Had buried long his hopes, no more to rise,
> Pleasure's palled victim ! Life abhorring gloom
> Wrote on his faded brow, cursed Cain's unresting doom."

This power of passion to coerce reason has a

remarkable illustration in the case of GEORGE
WACHS, a German youth, who was apprenticed
to one Schneeweisser, a carpenter, at Solling.
This lad, the son of a small farmer, lived an
irreproachably-moral life till his eighteenth year,
when he became dissolute in his habits. He then
grew wanton, riotous, disorderly, and lazy; fond
of dress, and excessively vain.

On the eve of a public festival, this unhappy
lad fell into the company of a young man who
ostentatiously displayed a watch. Wachs, who
did not own a watch himself, suddenly conceived
a desire to do so. This desire rapidly grew into
an irresistible passion. Happening to enter a shoemaker's house, shortly after, to have his boots
mended, his eye lighted on that gentleman's
watch, which hung upon a nail in the wall beside
him. Just at that moment the shoemaker's wife
went out to market, and the children also left
the house to play in the garden. Wachs and the
shoemaker were alone. Impelled by his passion
to obtain a watch, the dissolute youth stole behind
his victim, and, striking him with a large hammer

on the temple, he killed him with a single blow. The wife returning shortly after, he murdered her also, lest she should betray him. To make discovery impossible, he killed "Little Michael," their son, and, as he supposed, their daughter, Catherine; who, however, subsequently recovered from her wound, and became the principal witness on his trial, which resulted in his decapitation by the sword.*

This is an extreme case, I admit, but it is valuable because it shows the fearful weakness of the man who once surrenders himself to the control of his propensities. It proves the trite but terrible truth, that there is no propensity which may not, when fostered by indulgence and favored by circumstances, grow into an irresistible passion, and hurry a man into the commission of monstrous crimes!

Another consequence of vice is the remorseful sense of shame, the guilty consciousness of self-

---

* See Narratives of Remarkable Criminal Trials. From the German of Anselm Ritter Von Feuerbach. Harper's edition.

degradation which overwhelms a young sinner. No sooner does he quit the infamous haunts of slaughtered innocence, and retire to the silence and the solitude of his chamber, than the image of his offense fastens upon his soul with all the tenacity with which ghoul and vampire are said to seize their prey. Who can tell the full bitterness of the young soul when reviewing its fall? The first violated Sabbath, or the first revel over the foaming wine-cup, or the first forbidden visit to the theater, the gambler's den, or the chamber of pollution, is followed by fierce self-reproaches, by unutterable regrets, by unspeakable stingings of conscience! With eyes downcast, hands clasped, and heart burning with anguish, the young man cries, "What have I done? Fool that I was, to listen to my tempters! What would my mother feel, if she knew my guilt? How can I ever look her in the face again, with this spot upon my soul? And O, if I should die in this guilty state! Alas! alas! I am undone!"

Thus do showers of burning thoughts fall upon his tortured soul with a severity which Coleridge compares to "needle-points of frost drizzling on a bald and feverish head." At length, with many a weak resolve to go no further in sin, he falls asleep. When he awakes, his terrors have departed. His propensities resume their sway, and he is hurried into blacker transgressions. By persevering in sin, he succeeds in hardening his conscience, till, for the time being, it ceases its terrors, and he sins on, "neither fearing God nor regarding man."

It is impossible to predict with certainty the specific mode by which an abandoned youth will reach the goal of ruin. Neither can it be told how long or how short will be his career. These things depend upon which propensity plays the tyrant over him; upon his opportunities for self-indulgence; upon his caution; upon many circumstances entirely beyond his control. But this much is certain: without speedy and effectual reform, HIS RUIN IS A MORAL CERTAINTY! How long it will be delayed, or in what form it will come, can not be predicted; but come it will, as surely as consequence succeeds to cause. For, *"though hand joined in hand, the wicked shall not go unpunished."*

Sometimes the ruin of a vicious youth overtakes him with the swiftness of an arrow, as the following fact will show. A fine, noble-looking youth — I will call him REGINALD — who had been piously trained, left his virtuous home to dwell in a large city. At first, every returning Sabbath beheld him an attentive listener in the house of God. But he fell into the company of the wicked; resisted their seductions a while, then yielded. He now forsook the church for the haunts of pleasure. Being ardent in his temperament, he partook eagerly of every form of sin. The flowing bowl, the theater, the gambling-saloon, the brothel, witnessed his fiery zeal in the ways of iniquity. But his race was short—his ruin terrible and speedy. *Three months* of guilty abomination sufficed to break down his physical constitution, and to lay his fine and noble form, a pitiful wreck, upon a dying bed. Let us take our stand beside him, and witness the end of a vicious life.

Mark his pale, attenuated face, covered with blotches, and distorted with the combined ago- nies of mind and body! How languid and dull are his glassy eyes! How painful his breathing! How that deep, hoarse cough incessantly racks his almost fleshless body! But hearken! some one raps at the door! See! the patient turns his eyes upon the intruder, with an expression of horror; then nervously clutching the bedclothes, he buries his head beneath the folds, and obstinately refuses all conversation!

Who is this visitor? His countenance com- bines commanding dignity with bland benevo- lence, and is any thing but offensive. Why, then, does the dying youth feel so disturbed by his presence? The reader will understand the rea- son, when he learns that he is Reginald's former pastor. His person revives the memory of purer days, and the guilty sufferer dares not to see him.

As Reginald will not converse, the good man offers a prayer, and, with his hand upon the door- latch, is preparing to leave. But now the dying victim uncovers his face, sits up in the bed, and cries,

"Stop a minute, sir!"

The pastor returns to the bedside. The sufferer's effort has exhausted his strength, and he has fallen back upon the pillows. As the minister bends over to catch his words, Reginald throws his skinny arms around his neck, and whispers, with awful emphasis, "I'M LOST!" Then, burying himself once more beneath the clothes, he resolutely refuses all further conversation. Reader, that utterance was his last, for he never spoke again! How awfully did that dear, ruined young man verify the saying of Solomon: "*With her much fair speech she causeth him to yield; with the flattering of her lips she forced him. He goeth after her straightway, as an ox goeth to the slaughter, or as a fool to the conviction of the stocks; till a dart strike through his liver. As a bird hasteth to the snare, and knoweth not that it is for his life!*"

There can be no doubt that such cases as this are far from being rare. Vice is a swift and sure destroyer, and a youth who embraces her is as the early flower exposed to the untimely frost. Those who have perished thus are named "Legion;" for they are many—enough to convince every novice that he has no security that he shall escape a similar fate.

Nor is it always by disease alone a young profligate finds a speedy and fatal termination to his career. Ruin is a Briareus with many hands. As some large rivers debouch to the ocean through many mouths, so has vice many streams that lead to death. The vices, like the Furies, are sisters, and no man can espouse one without admitting the rest into his home: hence, no sinner can tell whither his besetting sin will conduct him. Let the following *fact* illustrate and enforce this thought:

A young man, whom I will name ARTHUR, nineteen years of age, educated, handsome, of fascinating manners, and manly spirit, visited a certain city in search of business. There he unhappily fell into dissolute society, and began to run the giddy rounds of deep dissipation. A few months served to exhaust his finances and to run him into debt. A bill lay upon his table, one day, which he was required to pay the next morning. Not knowing what to do, he took the fatal step of selling an opera-glass, which he had borrowed from a gay friend, and thus paid the bill. His friend called for the glass. Arthur, though much confused, frankly confessed his fault, and promised to obtain funds from home to remunerate the loser. But his quondam friend had the heart of a Shylock, and hurried the astonished and mortified young man to the police court, charging him with the crime of stealing the opera-glass. After a summary hearing, he was committed for trial, and immured in jail.

He was placed in a cell with another prisoner— a young man. As soon as he found himself there, the full measure of his disgrace rose before his agonized mind. Casting himself to the ground, he cried to his fellow-prisoner, in tones of exquisite anguish,

"Cut my throat! kill me! trample me to death!

My parents! How can I ever look them in the face again ?"

He grew more and more excited, beat his head upon the stone floor with such violence that his companion seized him and called lustily for aid. The turnkey came, and judging from his paroxysms that he was in a fever, called for a physician, who pronounced him to be in imminent danger of dying. A distinguished philanthropist was sent for, who bailed the young man, and conveyed him to his own residence. Touched by the affectionate kindness of this benevolent man, the youth stated that his father was a clergyman, and his relatives wealthy. The peril of life being very great, his generous protector wrote an account of the sad affair, and summoned the father to his son's death-bed. While the letter was on its way, during an interval of calmness, he was asked if he would not like to see his father once more.

"O no! Let me die rather—kill me! I have brought dishonor upon his gray hairs, and how can I look upon his face again? Let me die, but have pity on my poor father !"

The father arrived. "Your father is below, waiting to see you," said his attendant.

The sufferer uttered a piercing groan, covered his face, and exclaimed,

"I can't see him! I can't—I can't! Speak to him for me; tell him I died—"

Here the venerable father entered, and stood transfixed with agony beside his dying son! What a scene! That noble boy, that cherished child, polluted with profligate habits, disgraced by crime, dying of mental torture—and that aged minister, that white-haired father, gazing unutterable pity, and pierced with anguish that beggars description! Can aught of misery be fancied more exquisite or excruciating? Yet, young man, that scene grew out of just such indulgences as you are feverishly panting to enjoy. Pause, I beseech you! Examine well the ground you long to tread. Inquire seriously if you are prepared to receive the consequences before you set the cause in motion. For as surely as you abandon virtue, sooner or later, "*The Lord shall give thee a trembling heart, and failing of eyes, and sorrow of mind, and thy life shall hang in doubt before thee, and thou shalt fear day and night. In the morning thou shalt say, would God it were evening; and in the evening, would God it were morning: for the fear of thine heart wherewith thou shalt fear; and for the sight of thine eyes which thou shalt see!"*

But a vicious life does not always come to so sudden and speedy a conclusion. God often suffers the sinner to fill up a *large* measure of sin, and to place the hour of retribution far off. When this is the case, the heart grows stout and bold. The conscience becomes blind, and dead to feeling. The fear of God is entirely cast off. Religion is treated as a fable. The Gospel is trampled under foot, and the man, made brutish, vile, and abominable, becomes *"a vessel of wrath fitted to destruction!"*

Now, I doubt not that the reader, in the plenitude of his self-confidence, has thought himself strong enough to enter on vicious pursuits, without committing those crimes which destroy reputation and lead to the prison. Well, he may stop

short on the brink. The thing is abstractly possible—just as a man *might* gallop a furious horse
down a steep path which terminates at a precipice
with a deep gulf beneath, and rein up his beast
at the very brink. But the peril would be so imminent, none but a madman would venture on the
experiment. So you may give passion the reins
till it carries you close to *crime*, and then resume
the bridle and save yourself. The risk is fearful,
however, and no prudent youth will dare to
incur it.

There are two facts which the unitiated young
sinner does not duly weigh. The first is, that
vice so deadens the moral sense, and so blinds
the mind, that *crime* does not appear the same
horrible thing as it did in the happy days of innocence. The second is, that the cost of illicit
pleasures exceeds the resources of most young
sinners. Once taken in their net, the foolish
youth is too weak to break the entangling meshes.
He *must* sin on: hence, he *must* have money.
Honorably he can not obtain it. The card-table,
the dice-box, billiards, lotteries, and other modes

of gambling, invite him to replenish his empty purse by their aid. The poor dupe tries, and finds himself fleeced and reduced to extremities. What is to be done? He has gone too far to retrace his steps. Yet, he must extricate himself in some way. The tempter whispers the guilty thought of robbing his employers. He starts back at the mere idea of such an act. But his debts are pressing upon him, his habits are expensive, his passions imperious. Again the tempter whispers in his heart. The idea haunts him by day and by night, till by familiarity its malign aspect loses its power to terrify. The attempt is resolved on, but on some specious mental pretense of afterward restoring what is to be taken. The opportunity offers itself. The deed is done, and the young sinner trembles to find himself a thief! Gradually his fears depart. Finding himself undetected, he steals again, till it becomes his settled practice to embezzle the property of his employer, in order to pay the expenses of his lusts. Discovery comes at length, and he who began his career by going to a theater, ends it in the shame and ignominy of a prison. As said a weeping and disconsolate mother, one day, to a minister, who, seeing her distress, asked, "What is the matter with you, madam?"

"O my child! my child! He is just committed to prison! O, that theater! He was a virtuous, kind youth, till the theater proved his ruin."

Nor was this woman's son an exception. The commissioners of the Pentonville prison, in Great Britain, affirm that ninety-five per cent. of the criminals in British jails were made so by vices, whose cost, exceeding their incomes, led to the perpetration of crime! How dangerous a thing is vice! Who is safe, when so many have fallen? Young reader, beware! Crime and imprisonment are the legitimate consequences of sinful indulgences: hence, if you shudder at the idea of being the inmate of a jail, beware of the first step in the way thereto.

Would you know somewhat of the effects of vice upon that physical constitution which it

does not immediately destroy? Then, mark that
man who is slowly toiling along the street, leaning upon his cane. With what difficulty he drags
one emaciated leg after the other! How thin
and angular are his form and features! Every
slow movement proclaims his excessive languor.
There is no health or vigor in his motion. His
breath is short. A weak, hollow cough distresses
him. His face is pale as death. His eyes,
covered with a glassy film, have no expression.
His whole appearance is that of abject misery.
But see, he has seated himself on that door-step
to rest! Let us question him as to his sufferings. Hearken, as in a low, husky voice, he
details his list of pains! "My head," he says,
"is always dizzy. I have a constant headache.
My memory is gone, and I can not confine my
mind to any subject of thought. I find it
difficult to apprehend an idea; labor or study
are loathsome to me. My strength is all gone.
My back, my sides, my limbs are in constant
pain, and my mind and body are sinking into
utter ruin!"

This is terrible. Suppose we ask, " What brought you into this state, friend ?"

Hear his reply, as he gazes upon us with a look of unutterable despair: *"I brought it all upon myself,* BY INDULGENCE IN SOLITARY AND SOCIAL VICES !"

Sad confession ! Nevertheless, my picture is from life. Vice makes war upon every function in the human body. The brains, the heart, the lungs, the liver, the spine, the limbs, the bones, the flesh, every part and faculty, are overtaxed, worn, weakened by the terrific energy of passion and appetite 'loosed from restraint, till, like a dilapidated mansion, the "earthly house of this tabernacle" falls into "ruinous decay."

I have already described the tumult awakened in the conscience of a young profligate by his first steps in the wrong direction; and, also, the agony, despondency, and misery occasioned by a discovery of his inability to break his self-imposed bonds. The former state of mind is usually followed by one of hardened indifference, till the latter commences. But this settled gloom, bad as it is, does not compare in its terribleness with the more fearful sufferings of his heart, when, toward the close of earthly existence, he is visited by the horrors of REMORSE, that frowning "rock that stops the current of our thought to God." Then,

> "The past lives o'er again
> In its effects, and to the guilty spirit
> The ever-frowning present is its image."

Then he understands the truth of Coleridge's striking lines:

> "Just heaven instructs us, with an awful voice,
> That conscience rules us, e'en against our choice.
> Our inward monitress to guide and warn,
> If listened to; but, if repelled with scorn,
> At length, as dire remorse, she reappears,
> Works in our guilty hopes and selfish fears,
> Still bids *remember* and still cries *too late*,
> And while she scares us goads us to our fate."

How much a sinner suffers from the sting of remorse, no pen can describe, no heart can fancy. "The agonies inflicted by the wolf that fed on the life-stream of the Spartan, the poison injected by the tooth of the viper, or the three-fanged sting of the scorpion, are as nothing when contrasted with the stings of an accusing conscience. Most truly has an American writer observed that there is no manliness or fortitude can bear up under the horrors of guilt. The thing is done; yet it rises, in all its vivid coloring, to the soul that has incurred it, overwhelming it with remorse and despair. The reproaches of conscience, once thoroughly aroused, can neither be silenced nor borne. No human spirit can sustain its energies under such a burden, when it really comes." Hence, notorious criminals, who have denied their crimes while stretched on racks and wheels, have subsequently surrendered themselves to justice through the fiercer torments of remorse. To confirm these remarks, I submit two or three confessions which fell from the lips of some wretched victims of remorse.

"I would die — I dare not die! I would live — I dare not live! O, what a burden is the hand of an angry God!" exclaimed the terrified Viscount Kenmuir, in his dying moments.

"Is your mind at ease?" asked Dr. Turton, of the departing Oliver Goldsmith, as he lay tossed with an anguish deeper than what his disease occasioned.

"No, IT IS NOT!" was the sad reply of the once gay and jolly author of "The Deserted Village," as, deserted of God, he fought his last battle with Death.

"I feel the weight of God's wrath burning like the pains of hell within me, and pressing on my conscience with an anguish which can not be described!" cried the apostate Francis Spira, when writhing in the agonies of death.

"My dear, you appear as if your heart were breaking," said a weeping lady to her dying infidel husband, whose distress appeared to be unendurable.

"Let it break! Let it break! but it is hard work to die!" he replied. Then directing a glance toward heaven, he cried, "Lord, have mercy! Jesus save!" and died.

14

Now, all this is most shocking to contemplate. What, then, must its endurance be? And it is nothing more than the harvest gathered from a vicious life. Every illicit enjoyment is a seed of such torment as this. The guilty revel over the wine-cup, the scoff at religion, the sneer at piety, the hilarity of the dance, the embrace of lust, the violated Sabbath, the profane expression, are each and all the substances of those images which rise up, grim and ghostly, to torment the remorseful sinner. If, then, my dear young friend, you tremble at the consequences, shun the cause—sow not the seed—touch not the sin—stray not from the side of virtue! But if you will, despite of all warning voices, seek to know the mysteries of vice, then I say to you, in the language of inspiration,

"*Rejoice, O young man, in thy youth; and let thy heart cheer thee in the days of thy youth, and walk in the ways of thine heart, and in the sight of thine eyes;* BUT KNOW THOU THAT FOR ALL THESE THINGS GOD WILL BRING THEE INTO JUDGMENT. THEREFORE, PUT AWAY EVIL FROM THY

FLESH!" Seek the aids of pure religion. Cleave to purity, quiet, and virtue, and thus you "*shall dwell safely, and shall be quiet from fear of evil*"

CHAPTER XI.

VICE AND ITS SEDUCERS

"Come home! there is a sorrowing breath
  In music since ye went;
And the early flower-scents wander by,
  With mournful memories blent.
The tones in every household voice
  Are grown more sad and deep,
And the sweet word, *brother*, wakes a wish
  To turn aside, and weep."

THESE exquisite lines, by MRS. HEMANS, give
a beautiful expression to those tender affections which plead with every young man to maintain his affinity with home and its virtuous pleasures.   They show the strength of those restraining
influences with which God would fain hold the
young sinner back from vice.   All its love and all
its friendship plead with him, weep over him, wait
for him.   Though by his profligacy he has dug a
gulf between it and himself, yet it maintains an

unalienated regard, and with open arms and unutterable emotion, cries, "Come home!" Holy love! Affection almost divine! How strange, that the voices of lust and infamy should ever exert a more controlling power over a young man's spirit than these loving voices of home!

Yet so it is in every instance of youthful delinquency. The false-hearted victims of foul iniquity sway his soul, and render him deaf to the pleadings of his best and purest friends. His foolish heart yields itself up to vicious seducers, whose only aim is his destruction. A fashionable popinjay, a foppish blackguard, a gambler, a filthy harlot, is permitted to silence and push aside a venerable father, a fond mother, a pure sister, and a noble brother. This fact alone exhibits the hatefulness of vice, and should cause a young man to seriously pause before placing a foot on the accursed threshold of its infamous temple. To describe the seducers to vice, and to caution my reader against them, are my aims in this chapter.

Bad books and impure pictures are among the first corrupting instrumentalities which debase a

young mind. With the former may be ranked the
innumerable novels which are perpetually issuing
from unprincipled presses; all kinds of amorous
poetry; and a class of filthy books, pretending to
be medical, physiological, and instructive, while
in reality they are only disgusting stimulants to
unholy, prurient desires. Among the latter are
those engravings and paintings, whether in books
or papers, or on the covers of snuff-boxes, etc.,
which, from their immodesty, are calculated to
defile the mind and call the latent depravity of
the heart into action. These vile productions of
misdirected art the young man who values his
moral character must refuse to see. If they are
brought under his notice, he must resolutely turn
away his eyes from gazing upon them; for as sure
as he takes pleasure in them, he will be undone.
So of novels; they must be rejected with invincible determination.

But are all novels to be eschewed? Are not
some of them pure, both in style and tendency?
To this last question I reply, it is true that some
novels are better than others; in themselves they

may be unspotted. Yet in one point they do harm; they create a taste for fictitious reading. This taste soon acquires the intensity of a passion. The mind acquires a craving for excitement, and thus the youth, who begins by reveling among the splendid paintings of SIR WALTER SCOTT'S pen, or by subjecting himself to the quiet enchantment of FREDERIKA BREMER'S spirit, will speedily seek the works of more impassioned authors. He will hasten from DICKENS to JAMES, from James to BULWER, from Bulwer to AINSWORTH, from him to EUGENE SUE, and finally he will steep his polluted mind in the abominations of that Moloch among novelists, PAUL DE KOCK. By this time he is ready for destruction. By venturing in the pleasant ripple, he has been tempted to sport in the heaving breakers, till, caught by the resistless under-current, he is borne out to sea, and meets a premature death. How much better to have avoided the ripple! Young man, beware of reading your first novel!

But, alas! this counsel is probably too late! You are already under the spell of the charmer, and can hardly tolerate these censures! Not that you have no doubts concerning the effects of such reading; but you *love* it, passionately love it! You demand proof of the evil charged on these works.

Such proof is to be found in the experience of all novel-readers. Every such person knows that they *corrupt the heart, through the imagination.* They portray persons, characters, and scenes, to the imagination, which, being viewed there, inevitably bestir the lowest propensions of poor, fallen nature. The thief, the blasphemer, the skeptic, the seducer, the gambler—ideal wretches, whose actual presence in our home would be deemed a disgrace—are freely introduced into the "chambers of imagery," and permitted to utter all their filthy conversation, and to do their disgusting deeds, directly before the mind. Can this be done with impunity? Nay! As well might one hope to handle melted pitch and avoid defilement; for the imagination can not be polluted by vile images, without causing the heart to give forth depraved eruptions.

These eruptions may not take place at once.

They may delay to show themselves for a time; but the igniting spark is there, and only awaits a proper combination of circumstances to break forth. "Behold a fire smoldering and slumbering amid a heap of cinders. For a time it makes no progress; it dwells in darkness. One would suppose it had made up its mind for extinction. But judge not too hastily. The mass around has been penetrated by the heat, and prepared for its function. The fire has been blending itself with the cinders, and is ready to break out. Stir them once more. Clear them for the draught. Touch them once more, and the whole will break out into a conflagration." Thus it is with pernicious images in the mind. Their influence permeates the spirit. They fire the heart; they prepare the senses. Then comes the guilty opportunity, and the breath of the tempter. The spark ignites. The soul is in a blaze of passion. The sin is committed. The deed is done; and guilt binds its fearful burden upon the conscience, with chains of triple steel.

DANTE has delicately described the sad result

of inflaming the heart through such vile books. In his imaginary journey through perdition, he describes his interview with PAOLO and FRANCESCA, an Italian lord and lady, who were put to death for the crime of adultery. After questioning the guilty lady concerning her sin, he gives the following lines as her answer to his inquiries. She says:

> " One day
> For our delight we read of Lancelot,°
> How him love thralled. Alone we were, and no
> Suspicion near us. Ofttimes by that reading
> Our eyes were drawn together, and the hue
> Fled from our altered cheek. But at one point
> Alone we fell.
> °   °   °   °
>   The *book and writer both*
> *Were* GUILT's *purveyors*. In its leaves that day
> We read no more."

The poet has shown, in this exceedingly-delicate passage, how a bad book became the instrument of an evil which cost the virtue and lives

---

° The hero of the old romance. He was one of the knights of the famous Round Table.

of the parties. With these views before him, will any young man, who sets the least value upon his innocency, dare to run the risk of losing it for the sake of the dangerous pleasure afforded by a corrupting book? If my young reader has already fallen into the snare, let him glance a moment at his peril, and escape while he may. For though, by some extraordinary measure of Providence, he *may* escape from utter ruin, yet he can not, by any possibility, avoid a high degree of hurt to his intellectual and moral nature. If, as TENNYSON has written, every man may truly say,

"I am a part of all that I have met;"

and if, as a writer in the Edinburgh Review beautifully remarks, "the stream will make mention of its bed—the river will report of those shores which, sweeping through many regions and climes, it has washed—then those currents of thought whose sources lie afar off" must be affected by the quality of the books through which it has run. The character must be more or less modified by the intellectual companionships of its early years.

Reject, therefore, with virtuous horror, every book, however fascinating or eloquent it may be, which tends to stimulate any evil propensity of your nature. Turn from it with disgust. It is a seducer of virtue, a pander to vice — an evil to be abominated, shunned, and dreaded.

Next to bad books comes *the influence of abandoned companions.* To seduce the innocent into a depth of iniquity as deep as that into which themselves have fallen, is the delight of bad men. Some do this for what they may gain of their unhappy dupe; others, for the fiendish pleasure it affords a depraved heart to see itself equaled in wickedness by kindred minds. Mind, like air, seeks its equilibrium. Hence, a virtuous youth may settle it as an indisputable fact, that his guilty companions will either drag him down to their level, or he must raise them up to his. Otherwise, they must cease intercourse.

It is rare that a novice in iniquity falls at once into the hands of finished seducers. Novices are usually reached at first by young men of their own age, who have recently taken their first degrees in glaring sin. The merry, roistering jollity of such sinners, their gaycty of spirit, their apparent happiness, the glowing descriptions they give of their festivities, the sly hints they throw out at the *greenness* of the uninitiated, the half-playful, half-earnest banterings with which they greet their bashful excuses for not joining in their vices, are the first seductive influences which usually reach young men from the wicked. By these means they learn to love their society; they lose their relish for the purity and quiet of home; they feel mortified at their ignorance of iniquitous practices; till, surrendering themselves to the guidance of these children of sin, they take costly lessons for themselves in Sabbath-breaking, in drinking revels, and in forbidden visits to that pandemonium of all evil, the theater.

Here, then, young man, is the turning-point of your destiny. When your heart first feels enchanted by young men whom you know to be the occasions of grief to their friends and of suspicion to their employers, your danger is imminent and extreme. The fact that you fail to discern the full enormity of their practices, is the sign that you are marked for destruction. There is a certain bird which prepares its prey for its talons, by fluttering over its head and blinding its eyes with the sand with which it previously covers itself. The brilliant devices of gay sinners, like sand, blinding your eyes to the consequences of sin, fit you to be their prey. Now, therefore, or never, is your opportunity to escape. Break away at once from their snares, or you are undone. Once abandoned to their influence, you are lost. They will lead you from sin to sin, till you are as highly accomplished in the arts of vice as the worst. Remember that "evil companions will blight in you the delicate flower of innocence, which diffuses itself around you as a sweet perfume."

Among the more finished seducers to vice are the gambler, the libertine, and the skeptic. These are walking pestilences, less merciful to their victims than the howling wolf to the bleating lamb. Woe unto the young man who falls into their power!

The *gambler* is usually a drunkard. He needs

the stimulus of spirits to sustain the excitements of the card-table. He has no principles of honor, or integrity; for cheating is his trade. He has no pity. His heart is as adamant. He will fleece his victim of the last penny he has in the world, though he knows the poor dupe has a starving family at home, and will either go forth from his den to become a robber, or to rush unbidden into the presence of his God. He has the body of a man, but the spirit of a devil. It is his meat and his drink to destroy and ruin his fellow-creatures. Yet this is the man who will greet a young man with smiles and with flattery; who will praise his skill, laud his courage, and predict his success at the gaming-table. This is the man to whom silly youths surrender themselves. Will you, my reader, study this etching well? Imprint it on your memory, and, if ever you are unhappily lured into his den, call it up in its freshness, and let it hold you back from becoming either his victim or his representative.

The *libertine* is a beast in human form. He is a man enslaved in chains, self-wrought and riveted by his own hands. The dignity of his manhood is obliterated. Every noble human quality, every elevating attribute of character, and every God-like trait, are defaced, blurred, and buried underneath the teeming vices of sensuality. His very aspect proclaims his deep degradation. In place of the calm intellectuality which robes a virtuous countenance with grace and splendor, is the downcast, expressionless look of the mere animal. His neglected and stunted soul, long enchained, like a galley-slave, by the tyrannical senses and passions, seems to have lost its high powers of reasoning and willing, and to tamely endure a bondage it can not escape. A corrupt and loathsome wretch, the libertine sins on, till his filthy body tumbles, a heap of ruins, into an oblivious grave.

Do such disgusting creatures as these ever become the seducers of virtuous young manhood? They do. For even they can lure with the tongue. They can draw inflaming pictures to the fancy; they can sneer at the ignorance of innocence; they can persuade the unwary youth to venture across the threshold of infamy. They find infamous pleasure in the overthrow of virtuous resolve. Woe, therefore, to him who dares to venture into their society! They begin their efforts by hints, and, as TUPPER properly remarks,

" Hints shrewdly strown mightily disturb the spirit,
   The sly suggestion toucheth nerves, and nerves contract the fronds,
   And the sensitive mimosa of affection trembleth to its root."

Libertines understand this principle. Hence, they are careful to captivate by sly inuendoes, and not to disgust by gross description. When their victim is sufficiently blunted in his moral sensibility, and excited in his passion, they lead him, half-reluctant, half-willing, into the path of the "strange woman." The word of God graphically describes the unhappy simpleton who suffers himself to be thus beguiled:

"I beheld," says the wise man, "among the simple ones; I discerned among the youths A YOUNG MAN VOID OF UNDERSTANDING, passing through the street near her corner; and he went

15

the way to her house, in the twilight, in the evening, in the black and dark night."

How striking is this picture! How lifelike its penciling of the young man who is laboring to break down the last bulwark of virtue in his soul! His already-polluted mind, brought into subjection by the baser passions, impels him, when the sun is down, to venture within the precincts of iniquity. He walks around the place of vile resort, as if inviting the temptation of the wretched creatures who abide there. Later in the evening, he repeats his walk; just as the moth returns to the flame of the lamp. At length the hour most fitted for crime arrives—"the black and dark night." And continues Solomon, "Behold there met him a woman with the attire of an harlot, and subtile of heart. So she caught him and kissed him, and with an impudent face said unto him: 'Come, let us take our fill of love until the morning.' With her much fair speech she caused him to yield, with the flattering of her lips she forced him. HE GOETH AFTER HER STRAIGHTWAY, AS AN OX GOETH TO THE

SLAUGHTER, OR AS A FOOL TO THE CORRECTION OF
THE STOCKS !"

Such is the process of ruin. Let the reader
study this description till he feels an irrepressible
loathing toward that impudent seducer of virtue,
and a terrible dread of standing in the place of
that simple youth. For, awful indeed is the fate
that awaits him. His sin will cause "*a dart to
strike through his liver.*" The house he enters is
"THE WAY TO HELL, GOING DOWN TO THE CHAM-
BERS OF DEATH." The feet of the woman he
follows "GO DOWN TO DEATH; HER STEPS TAKE
HOLD ON HELL." Her power is so resistless, that
"*none that go to her return again: neither take
they hold of the paths of life.*" She binds them
fast in her bonds, till they "*mourn at the last
when* THEIR FLESH AND THEIR BODY ARE CON-
SUMED !"

Are not these fearful descriptions sufficient to
call a vow from your heart, young man, never to
fall into such hands? or to induce you, if you are
deceived by some diabolical wretch, as was a young
man I will call PETER PERCY, and led to the snare

to burst it and depart? Peter was conducted by a designing companion into a house of ill repute, whose character he did not even suspect? His pretended friend led him into a chamber, introduced him to a poor, fallen creature, and, turning away, locked the door, and left him, as he thought, a sure prey to the charmer. But virtue was strong in Peter's soul. He saw his danger at a glance. To parley was to fall. Running to the window, he beheld a distance of several feet between him and the ground. To leap might make him lame for life. To refrain might spot his soul forever. What is a physical hurt, compared with moral pollution? Nothing. So thought Peter; and he leaped from the window to the ground unhurt. A noble and manly act. It probably saved Peter's body from destruction and his soul from hell. Young man, "go thou and do likewise!" Ever be ready to say to libertine or harlot, "How can I do this great wickedness, and sin against God?" Thus shall you *"find life, and obtain favor of the Lord."*

The *skeptic*, the third I named among the

finished seducers to vice, is usually a greedy de-
vourer of souls. Miserable, unprincipled, given
over to work iniquity, he has an appetite for ruined
souls as insatiable as the horse-leech or the grave.
Though every sentence he utters against God and
revelation stings his own soul like an adder, yet
he pours forth his proud and haughty blasphemies
in floods of irony, sarcasm, and jests at sacred
things. Furious in his temper, he brooks no
denial of his monstrous doctrines. A mere sci-
olist in reality, he makes a great show of knowledge by quoting a few passages he has picked up
from infidel books, and thus often confounds the
modest youth whom he assaults. Merciless as
a catamount, he would corrupt the purest human
mind on earth, though he knew it would thereby
be brought down to the misery of the hell whose
unceasing fires burn within his own bosom. His
grand instrument of seduction is contempt. He
sneers at truth, and then hypocritically asks his
intended victim if a man of sense and mind
can believe such nonsense. Thus, by degrees,
he induces young men to grow proud of their

imaginary superiority, and to feel ashamed of revealed truth. This accomplished, the remainder of his satanic task is easy; for as waters flow readily when the obstructing dam is demolished, so, when belief in God and revelation is shaken, sin flows unrestrained from the depraved heart.

Beware, then, of the skeptic! Keep away from his person. Would you inhale the breath of the pestilence? Would you rush into the folds of a serpent? Would you leap into the enraged ocean? Yet either of these things is as proper to be done as to place yourself under the influence of a skeptic! Shun his society, therefore. Be satisfied to know that the best thing infidelity ever did, even for its princes and champions, was to corrupt their lives, and fill them with unutterable remorse. " LORD HERBERT, HOBBES, LORD SHAFTSBURY, WOOLSTON, TINDAL, CHUBB, and LORD BOLINGBROKE, were all guilty of the vile hypocrisy of lying." ROCHESTER and WHARTON were profligates. Woolston was a gross blasphemer BLOUNT, a suicide. VOLTAIRE was noted for "impudent audacity, filthy sensuality, persecuting envy, base adulation," tyrrany and cruelty. ROUSSEAU was a thief, a liar, and a profligate.* Need I say more? With such historical examples before his eyes, what young man will dare to suffer a skeptic to throw his seductive influences around him? Surely my reader will flee from him as for his life

Evil companions are, therefore, to be totally avoided. Safety is to be purchased only at the price of entire abstinence from their society; for, as he who tastes his first glass of intoxicating drink has no security against becoming a drunkard, so he who finds a little delight in the society of partially-corrupted persons, has abandoned the ground of absolute safety. He is within a charmed circle. The incantation has begun. The demon of the circle is nigh. Soon will he present the bond by which the young dupe will sign away his virtue, his hopes, his soul. Beware, O beware, then, of every one of the seducers to vice! Reject the bad book; turn away from the

---

* See Horne's Introduction, chap. i, pp. 24-26.

vile picture; refuse your company to the wicked!
Seek God and his children; so shall you happily
escape the dangers of life, and win a crown of
eternal glory.

CHAPTER XII.

COURTSHIP AND MARRIAGE.

BEHOLD yonder mass of barren rock, without a tuft of moss or lichen upon its surface! The wind rises, and a cloud of dust fills the air. A portion of this dust lodges in the numerous interstices of the rock, and erelong a tiny tuft of moss, borne on the wings of the breeze, or dropping from a neighboring tree, falls into a crevice filled with dust, vegetates, spreads, and covers the rock with a carpet of green. The moss decays and grows again. The stratum increases. Other plants spring up from seeds wafted to the spot by the ever-changing wind. These grow and rot, thereby increasing the depth of the soil, till, in the progress of time, it acquires depth sufficient to nourish the noblest forest trees. These humble mosses also powerfully attract moisture from the clouds, which, trickling through every crevice, finds its way to the lowest nook, accumulates, becomes first a rivulet, then a brook, a cascade, a river. This, flowing into the ocean, forms clouds by evaporation, and once more falls to fertilize the earth.

Thus does an observant philosopher describe the great results which nature brings forth from small beginnings. Yet, how many never dream of consequences from a cloud of dust! It is too small a matter to awaken a thought. So of a myriad more of nature's labors. They are the workings of an invisible, omnipotent God—the necessary processes of the world's existence. But men pass blindly on, and see nothing in them sufficiently significant to arrest their attention.

There is a corresponding blindness concerning many of those human actions whose consequences reach far into the future of man's existence. The commencement of that affectionate intercourse between a youth and a maiden, called courtship, is an example. How little is thought of the first buddings of love between two young persons! By the parents it is often deemed a fitting subject for joke and laughter. The parties themselves, conscious chiefly of a mutual attraction, abandon themselves to romantic visions of future bliss, and to efforts to please each other. Little do they dream that from their gay and lightsome intercourse is to proceed a stream of exquisite delight, or of burning poison, running parallel, perhaps, with their immortal existence; yet so it is. A life of bitter, bitter anguish, or of as much happiness as is permitted to mortals on earth, lies inclosed in the but too lightly-esteemed state of courtship. Next to marriage, it is the gravest and most solemn affair relating to life this side the grave.

Erroneous views of courtship have their foundation in low and ignoble ideas concerning marriage itself. How is marriage regarded by most young men? Alas! is it not viewed chiefly as a legal method of gratifying the sexual appetite?—as "a means of sensual gratification"—for the mere physical purposes of the continuance of the race?"* With these views of marriage, is it at all surprising that the courtship which stands in so intimate a relation to it is carried on in a light, unworthy, and even impure spirit? Is it wonderful that the parties frequently violate the laws of modesty, and become guilty before God and man? Is it strange that moral and intellectual affinities and repugnances are overlooked and disregarded? Nay, the wonder is that these things are not more common.

Now, young man, I wish you, as a moral and intellectual creature, to open your eyes, and behold with grateful wonder the noble designs of God, which lie hidden beneath this question of marriage. True, it has a physical purpose to accomplish. By it our species are to be continued in the healthiest and purest manner. But running parallel with this is the higher, nobler, loftier design of developing the purest affections of the heart, and the loveliest excellences of our nature.

---

* See a recent work by Dr. Ware, called "Hints to Young Men on the True Relation of the Sexes."

As Dr. Ware has well said, "The permanent union of one man with one woman establishes a relation of affections and interests which can in no other way be made to exist between two human beings. Without it no individual can be considered as having answered the whole purpose of his existence—of having arrived at the full development of which he is capable. He is incomplete and imperfect. He has tendencies, capacities, powers for good, which have never been called out, which he may not know even to exist. Domestic life, and the domestic relations, are the essential element of human happiness and human progress, so far as our moral and spiritual character are concerned. From the relation of the sexes springs all that gives its charm, its grace, its true value to human intercourse. It creates the domestic circle. It gives origin to the sacred relation of husband and wife, parent and child, brother and sister, and those thousand endearing relations which arise from them. Strike out from the life of man all the hopes, interests, and motives which grow out of this relation, and what were left him but a cheerless, a desolate, and a merely brutal existence?"

These are just and elevating views of marriage. How superior to those "abject and licentious doctrines, destructive of the conjugal tie, which certain classes of infidels endeavor to spread abroad in the world! Reject, with horror and disgust, such hideous teachings! They would degrade you to the level of the brute." Indulge purer and holier opinions, and you will thus "give yourself no reason to blush before the chaste and faithful dove, nor degrade the sacred character imprinted on your brow by the finger of God." Your heart will give forth a pure affection, worthy of your exalted nature, and fit to be offered to the spotless maiden whose charms of heart and mind may attract you to her side. And remember, you can not entertain opposite opinions without debasing and degrading yourself and your betrothed, by the intercourse implied in courtship. Neither can your marriage be truly "honorable," unless it be contracted on these Scriptural and exalted principles.

With these opinions deeply impressed on his mind, a young man is prepared to commence a truly-virtuous and elevating courtship. Accidental, spontaneous, and thoughtless, as first intimacies between the sexes are apt to be, he will, nevertheless, be induced to pause and reflect before acquaintanceship ripens into a positive betrothal. Looking at the true ends of marriage, he will inquire if the lady, toward whom his love is blossoming, possesses those qualities of heart and intellect which are suited to answer those ends. If she does not, though he *may* yield to the impulses of his passion, yet he will be far more likely to hesitate, before soliciting her hand in marriage, than he would be if his views were of that degrading nature before animadverted upon. And if ever caution is needed, it is here.. Mistake is so easy. Undesigned duplicity is so natural. The lady, wreathed in smiles, and moving with cautious effort to conceal defects of temper and intellect, acquires an almost irresistible influence over his feelings. The still small voice of the better judgment whispers, "Beware!" It suggests the lack of one adornment, the excess of a particular defect, the absence of certain desirable qualities and attainments, in vain. The *heart* silences the cooler dictates of the mind; the question is put, the engagement made, the vows exchanged, the marriage celebrated, and the wretched parties learn, when too late, their unfitness for each other; and, too often, their subsequent life is miserable beyond description. Be careful, therefore, young man, at the very beginning. When a slight fondness arises in your heart toward any particular lady, hold it in check till you have time to discover what she is. If manifestly unfit, intellectually, morally, or socially to be your future wife, stifle your affection. Seek other society. The pain of such a resolution will bear no comparison with the agony consequent upon an imprudent marriage.

Most young men are chiefly charmed by what are termed accomplishments in young ladies. Thrumming a piano, working on beads or worsted, smattering bad French, and worse Italian, are arts regarded by the enraptured youth with strange admiration, and he pronounces the lady performer a paragon of all perfection. But he should remember that these things, pleasing and even beneficial as they are in their place, are miserable substitutes for more solid and indispensable qualities. For, as HANNAH MORE has well observed, "Though the arts which embellish life claim admiration, yet when a man of sense comes to marry, it is a companion he wants, and not an artist. It is not merely a creature who can dress and paint and sing; it is a being who can comfort and counsel him; one who can reason, and reflect, and feel, and judge, and act; one who can assist him in his affairs, soothe his sorrows, lighten his cares, purify his joys, and educate his children." She should be well versed in the household labors of baking, roasting, washing, cleaning, and sewing; otherwise she is as unfit to be a wife as "a shoemaker would be to navigate a man-of-war across the Atlantic." Therefore,

"Take heed that what charmeth thee is real, nor springeth of thine own imagination:

And suffer not trifles to win thy love, for a wife is thine unto
    death;

The harp and voice may thrill thee—sound may enchant thine
    ear,

But consider thou, the hand will wither, and the sweet notes turn
    to discord;

The eye so brilliant at even may be red with sorrow in the
    morning;

And the sylph-like form of elegance must writhe in the crampings
    of pain."

Seek for substantial as well as artistical excellences in her you would make your wife. She
should be *frugal*, not wasteful; for an extravagant wife will bring embarrassment, if not poverty
itself, into your habitation; her ambition for
costly dress, costly furniture, costly living, will
empty your purse, ruin your business, introduce
you to the insolvent debtor's court; or, worse than
all, it will install the demon of discontent by your
fireside. She must be *industrious;* for a lazy
woman is always fretful, odious, and disgusting.
Who could endure a yawning, slipshod, sauntering,
sleepy wife? She should be *grave and sober* in
her demeanor. The gay romp, the rattling, laugh

ing coquette, may be very amusing at a party, but she is usually dull at home. The gayest and liveliest in society are frequently the most unhappy by the quiet fireside. She must be *modest;* for "how beautiful is modesty! It winneth upon all beholders." A young woman who will permit an unchaste word or hint to be uttered to her, even from her betrothed, or will herself give utterance to an impure suggestion, is unworthy of your love. She is an unsafe person to be admitted within the sacred sphere of marriage. She must be *intelligent* and *sensible;* if otherwise, it will be very difficult to maintain that esteem for her which is the basis of genuine and lasting love. An ignorant, blundering, silly woman, is sure to expose her husband to incessant mortification, and to excite contempt and scorn in his breast toward her. She should be of a *cheerful and an amiable disposition,* since on nuisance is more intolerable than a scolding, complaining, contentious woman. You had better be chained to the galleys, or allied to the plague, than to be married to such a creature. And, as a final quality, your intended bride should possess a *pleasing countenance.* I do not say that she needs to be beautiful, but since she has to be your constant companion, there must be something attractive in her form and face, to insure the continuance of affection. Beware of a woman whose features express harshness, cynicism, surliness, or sourness. Such expressions written on the countenance are the unerring indications of a mind distempered, of an unamiable disposition, of an unhappy heart. Therefore, avoid all such, as you would shun the cholera. Seek one from whose countenance inward loveliness beams like the softened light from a transparent vase.

"Affect not to despise beauty: no one is freed from its dominion;

But regard it not a pearl of price; it is fleeting as the bow in the clouds.

If the character within be gentle, it often hath its index in the countenance—

The soft smile of a loving face is better than splendor that fadeth quickly."

Remember that the bond of marriage is as gyves of brass; and, therefore, you must prefer doing violence to your feelings rather than to rush blindfold into certain misery, which can terminate only with the life of one of the parties.

But, whenever you can find a lady possessing the characteristics I have enumerated, seek her society, and, if you can, win her pure affections. Such an association, viewed in the aspect already exhibited, next to religion, is the best and surest preserver of virtue in a young man. It will meet a want of his nature; it will give him an object to love; and, as ROUSSEAU observes, "Were I in a desert, I would find out wherewith in it to call forth my affections. If I could do no better, I would fasten them upon some sweet myrtle, or some melancholy cypress. I would love it for its shade, and greet it kindly for its protection. I would write my name upon it, and pronounce it the sweetest tree ·in all the desert. If its leaves withered, I would teach myself to mourn; and if it rejoiced, I would rejoice with it."

There is much of poetry in this, but there is also a great truth beautifully expressed. The mind must have something to love, or it will prey upon itself. But when it finds an object of sufficient worth "to lead it out of itself to live in and for another," then it has gained its counter-part, and develops itself in a most pleasing and happy manner. Therefore, I say, seek a suitable object for your affection, though years may elapse before you are in a condition to marry. TUPPER gives a reason for such a step, in his "Proverbial Philosophy." He says,

"They that love early become like-minded, and the tempter toucheth them not:
They grow up leaning on each other, as the olive and the
  vine."

True affection, founded upon genuine esteem, must lie at the basis of honorable and pure mar-riage. Without such holy love in both the parties, disgust and wretchedness will be the baleful fruit of their legal alliance; for

"He that shuts love out, in turn shall be
  Shut out from love, and on her threshold lie
  Howling in outer darkness."

But even love is not the sole prerequisite of a happy marriage. A young man may find it neces-sary to nip his affections in the bud, if the lady who attracts him is far above his rank in society. There is deep meaning in the poet's counsel, who says:

"Be joined to thine equal in rank, or the foot of pride will kick
  at thee;
And look not only for riches, lest thou be mated with misery."

If she is below your grade, providing she have high moral and mental qualities, her lowliness and poverty need not stand in the way of your affection, since marriage always raises or depresses the woman to the level of her husband. Marry not for money's sake. Such a union is an abomination before God, and a degradation to the parties. Better let your bride resemble the Greek maiden, who, when asked what fortune she should bring to her husband, nobly replied,

"I will bring him what gold can not purchase — a heart unspotted, and virtue without a stain, which portion is all that descended to me from my parents."

Neither, if *you* happen to have wealth, should you select a bride who is more influenced by your invested moneys and flourishing business than by pure affection.   There are women, of whom, to the disgrace of their sex, it may be said in the language of Byron,

" But pomp and power alone are woman's care,
    And where these are, light Eros finds a fare;
    Maidens, like moths, are ever caught by glare,
    And mammon wins his way where seraphs might despair."

Shun all such creatures.   You had better take a viper into your bosom.

Avoid, also, a skeptical woman.   In these days of ultraism and radicalism, there are many such " moral monsters," who, forgetful of the hope and faith we naturally expect from their sex, have broken loose from their God, from the holy Scriptures, and from the delicacy of woman's nature. Such unfeminine creatures brawl loudly against revelation, and even venture before the public as loquacious leaguers with Voltaire, Paine, and Abner Kneeland.   Such women are unfit for marriage   If they respect not the claims of God, nor heed the bonds which bind them to religion, how can they be expected to be faithful to the law which binds them to a husband?   Impossible!

infidel men have understood this. Hence, LORD CHESTERFIELD counseled his son to marry a woman of pious tendencies; and DR. BRAINARD mentions a very profane man, who expressed joy that he was not "to be linked to a female infidel," whom he heard question the truth of the Bible. These men, bad as they were in other respects, were right in their opinion of the unfitness of a skeptical woman to be a wife. Do you take heed, my young friend, and keep your affections from such. Celibacy is far better than wedlock at the altar of infidelity.

Be not in haste to wed. While early marriages are to be encouraged, if circumstances are favorable, it is the hight of folly, and often the first step to a long career of bitterness, for parties to marry without any reasonable prospect of comfortable support.

> "Marry not without means; for so shouldst thou tempt Providence;
> But wait not for more than enough; for marriage is the DUTY of most men."

This is excellent counsel. A young man should

wait till his income is sufficient, his business established, his resources somewhat certain. Marriage brings with it many expenses, and these increase with time; and a marriage without means will surely bring poverty and sorrow. Affection is a poor banker, a miserable purveyor, a wretched landlord. With *limited* means it may do well, since it stimulates industry, excites energy, and can invent many innocent devices to compel small resources to supply large wants. Prudence must be allowed to utter its cautions in this matter; and if you are prudent, young man, you shall do well.

In courtship, a young man should be stable. A marriage engagement is a solemn and a serious affair. It takes a deep hold on the heart of a young woman. Her first love is a holy thing. It becomes life and gladness to her spirit. But,

" If the love of the heart is blighted, it buddeth not again:
  If that pleasant song is forgotten, it is to be learnt no more;
  Yet often will thought look back, and weep over early affection;
  And the dim notes of that pleasant song will be heard as a
    reproachful spirit,

Moaning in Æolian strains over the desert of the heart,
When the hot siroccos of the world have withered its one oasis."

If these affecting lines are true to experience, what shall be said of a young man who sedulously seeks a young girl's love, till, in her trustful simplicity, she yields him her whole heart, and looks up to him as the future companion of her life, and then, *through sheer fickleness*, abandons her for another? Is he not cruel, heartless, and false? Does he not inflict a deadly wound on her spirit, from which she may never wholly recover? Does he not deserve the severest reprehension? He does; and be assured that no young man can be guilty of such reckless trifling with the female heart, without being subsequently visited by the retributions of an avenging Providence. His sin will "*find him out.*"

But what if his first promises were prematurely given, and further acquaintance convinces him that the lady's ill qualities are such as will certainly imbitter his life in the event of marriage? Is he then to consummate his courtship, and enter with open eyes upon an "ill-assorted" union?

To this I answer, certainly not, providing there is a discovery of positive unfitness, and not a mere excuse for instability. The parties had better suffer the pang of separation during courtship, than to be yoked to a heritage of misery and sorrow for life. But beware, lest mere fickleness leads you to imagine faults merely to furnish an excuse for the violation of your engagement! Prefer to keep your promise unbroken, if it be at all consistent with your hopes of happiness. The true remedy for such separations is prevention. Let your first advances be sufficiently cautious to enable you to judge of the lady's character before you enter on more familiar intercourse. And another means is, to treat your courtship as a serious part of your conduct. Carry it on in a manner consistent with the high purposes of marriage; not with silly gigglings and idle commonplaces. Seek to cultivate each other's tastes, to call forth ideas and modes of thought hitherto undeveloped. Aim to produce a spiritual union between yourselves. By this means the little things which usually separate betrothed parties will not disturb your intercourse.

You will be satisfied with each other, and fitted for the more intimate and sacred unity of the marriage state.

Against one disgusting practice, but too popular in many parts of the country, allow me to earnestly counsel you. I mean the habit of sitting up to a late hour of the night with your betrothed. While there can not be one reason urged in defense of this unchristian custom, there are serious objections against it. It injures health; it unfits for the duties of the next day; it has an impure aspect, and is a temptation to virtue. By all the decencies and proprieties of life, I beg you, young man, to have self-respect sufficient to set yourself heartily against it. Let your intercourse take place at proper hours, and under circumstances which favor you and yours in acquiring an affinity of tastes and opinions.

I can not, perhaps, close this chapter on courtship and marriage more profitably, than by giving the eccentric and celebrated William Cobbett's account of his courtship. He was a sergeant-major in a British regiment of foot, serving in

Canada, when he first met the lady who afterward
became his wife. She was the daughter of a
sergeant of artillery, so that in rank they were
pretty equally matched. He first met her in
company, and was forcibly struck with the beauty
of her countenance, and the marked propriety of
her behavior. He resolved to note her conduct,
and to study her character. A few mornings after
this first introduction, he took occasion to walk,
with one or two companions, past her father's
house. Although it was scarcely light, he saw
her at the door, cheerfully scrubbing out a wash-
tub on the snow. This confirmed his good opinion. Further observation being still more in her
favor, he made up his mind that she should be
his wife at a proper time. This purpose he never
dreamed of changing. It was settled in his mind,
and he treated her accordingly. Her father's
regiment being ordered to England, it was necessary for them to be separated. To show the
fixedness of his purpose, and the confidence he
had in her affection, he gave her the entire amount
of his savings—six hundred and fifty dollars—

bidding her use it, if necessary for her personal comfort, before his arrival in England. This confidence was not misplaced. Though over four years elapsed before she saw him again, and she had to work hard, as a house-servant, for a living, yet she remained true to her vows, and returned him every dollar of the money he had placed in her hands. He married her, and attributed much of his signal success in life to her very excellent qualities.

But, notwithstanding Mr. Cobbett's fidelity to his first promise of marriage, he narrowly escaped the guilt of its violation. His betrothed had been absent two years. He was rambling in the woods of New Brunswick, when he stumbled upon a clearing, with a farmer who offered him the hospitalities of his home. This sturdy backwoodsman had a daughter — aged nineteen — a finely-formed, blue-eyed girl, with long, light-brown hair. Young Cobbett was charmed. He repeatedly visited the place, mingled in the parties and merry-makings of the homestead; and, notwithstanding he felt conscious of being attracted by the young lady, and that she was also becoming interested in him, persisted to visit her, till the idea of parting grew exceedingly painful to both. Happily his sense of obligation was strong; and, wrong as he was in placing himself within the sphere of temptation, and in trifling with the affections of another, he remained faithful to his first vows. This wrong of indulging in the society of the lady of the woods he very ingeniously confesses, and bids others act more wisely and cautiously, lest they should lack the self-control which finally saved him from becoming a covenant-breaker. I join my counsel to his, and advise every young man, first, to exercise due caution before making a marriage engagement; secondly, having made it, to consider it inviolable, except under very extraordinary circumstances; thirdly, to defer his marriage till, in the opinions of his parents or judicious friends, the suitable time has arrived; and, finally, to enter the marriage state with pure, spiritual, and holy views, that it be a real blessing to him and his bride in both worlds.*

---

* For Counsels to the Married, see a recent work by the author, entitled "Bridal Greetings."

CONCLUDING NOTE.

AND now, dear young friend, I must bid you adieu. I have urged the practice of great principles upon your understanding and heart, that you may win the prize of a happy and successful life. I have stimulated you to be eminent in your profession, by the due observance of the great and holy truths revealed in the Divine word. Not that I consider success in this life to be the end of your existence. No! To glorify God, to attain his moral likeness, to diffuse enjoyment among your fellow-creatures — these are the grand aims of human life. But in reaching these aims — in grasping the greater — you will more surely reach the lesser than by any other method; for religion is the good genius of both worlds. This idea I have endeavored to illustrate in the preceding pages. Let me entreat you to seize it heartily and earnestly! Let it blend with all your thinkings. Allow it to mold your character, to govern

17

your conduct. Thus will you rise to usefulness and enjoyment on earth, and to a place in that moral firmament where the wise and good "SHALL SHINE AS THE STARS FOREVER AND EVER."

THE END.

www.ingramcontent.com/pod-product-compliance
Lightning Source LLC
Chambersburg PA
CBHW031420020726
47499CB00005B/1513